Ross felt his hea **when he saw t** **ground. Gemm** **lifeless, that he w** **arr** **aid to move.**

Then all of a sudden he was running towards her, slipping and sliding in his haste to reach her. He felt her breath on his skin. She was alive, and that was a miracle in itself.

'Gemma, can you hear me? Sweetheart, it's Ross. Can you open your eyes?'

There was no response at first, and then her lids slowly rose a fraction. 'Ross? How did you find me?' she whispered. She bit her lip and he saw her eyes fill with tears. 'I didn't think anyone would even notice I was missing, let alone come and look for me.'

'I noticed you were missing.' He smiled at her, uncaring what she might see in his eyes at that moment. He'd been through hell, and just to have her here, safe and sound, was the best thing that had ever happened to him.

He kissed her lightly on the forehead, hoping she understood what he was trying to say. Maybe it was too soon to tell her how he felt, but there was no point denying it. The thought that he might have lost her today was more than he could bear. Now all he had to do was convince her that it was *her* he loved…

Dear Reader

This is the second book in my *Dalverston Weddings* series, and it tells the bridegroom's story. The book begins the morning after Ross has learned that his wedding will no longer be taking place. Naturally, Ross is stunned by what has happened but, if he is honest, he is also relieved. Deep down he knows that he was getting married for the wrong reasons—although convincing his friends and family that he isn't about to fall apart seems like an impossible task! The only person he can talk to is bridesmaid and practice nurse Gemma Craven. As the days pass Ross finds himself increasingly drawn to Gemma, but is he in danger of making another mistake? Can he really be falling in love with Gemma so soon?

Both Ross and Gemma have a lot of issues to work through before they can find true happiness, and it was a fascinating process bringing them together. I really enjoyed their story and hope you do too. The next book in the series features the best man, Ben Nicholls, who makes a brief appearance in this book, too. It's one of the joys of writing a series like this—you really get to know your characters. I shall miss them all when the last book has been written.

If you would like to learn more about the background to this series then do visit my website: www.jennifer-taylor.com

Happy reading!

Love

Jennifer

THE GP's
MEANT-TO-BE
BRIDE

BY
JENNIFER TAYLOR

MILLS & BOON
Pure reading pleasure™

All the characters in this book have no existence outside the imagination of the author, and have no relation whatsoever to anyone bearing the same name or names. They are not even distantly inspired by any individual known or unknown to the author, and all the incidents are pure invention.

First published in Great Britain 2008
Harlequin Mills & Boon Limited,
Eton House, 18-24 Paradise Road, Richmond, Surrey TW9 1SR

© Jennifer Taylor 2008

ISBN: 978 0 263 86365 9

Set in Times Roman 10½ on 12¾ pt
03-1208-48951

Printed and bound in Spain
by Litografia Rosés, S.A., Barcelona

Jennifer Taylor lives in the north-west of England, in a small village surrounded by some really beautiful countryside. She has written for several different M&B series in the past, but it wasn't until she read her first Medical™ Romance that she truly found her niche. She was so captivated by these heart-warming stories that she set out to write them herself!

When she's not writing, or doing research for her latest book, Jennifer's hobbies include reading, gardening, travel, and chatting to friends both on and off-line. She is always delighted to hear from readers, so do visit her website at www.jennifer-taylor.com

Recent titles by the same author:

MARRYING THE RUNAWAY BRIDE*
THE SURGEON'S FATHERHOOD SURPRISE†
THEIR LITTLE CHRISTMAS MIRACLE

*Dalverston Weddings
†Brides of Penhally Bay

For The Wedding Party: Vicky and Jamie,
Kathy, Carl, Pauline, John, Nigel, Neil, Mark, Mel.
And last but never least, Bill.
Thank you all for an unforgettable day.

CHAPTER ONE

TODAY should have been his wedding day.

Ross Mackenzie sighed as he stared out of the bedroom window. Dawn was starting to break now, the first pale streaks of wintry light sliding over the top of the surrounding hills. He hadn't slept. He'd lain awake all night long, working out the best way to proceed. There were a lot of things he needed to do that morning. First and foremost on the list he would have to tell his mother that the wedding wouldn't be taking place. He wasn't looking forward to breaking the news to her because she was bound to be upset, but he would try to do it as gently as possible.

Next he would have to inform all the guests that the wedding had been called off. Some were travelling quite a distance so he would have to phone them as early as possible. Then there was the vicar—he would need to be informed, and the cars and the flowers would have to be cancelled, as well as the reception. The list seemed endless but Ross knew that he would work his way through it in his usual meticulous fashion. If he was honest, it wasn't the practicalities that worried him, but how he *felt*. Surely he should feel more than this sense of relief that Heather had decided not to marry him?

He swung round, impatient with himself. He should be glad that he wasn't standing here, feeling as though the world had caved in around him! Walking through to the en suite bathroom, he turned on the shower. Once he was dressed, he would set everything in motion. Granted, it would cause a stir once word got out and he wasn't looking forward to being the focus of so much gossip. However, he wasn't going to let it deter him. He would deal with what had happened the same way he dealt with everything else—calmly and rationally.

He grimaced as he stepped under the hot water because he knew that his reaction wasn't normal. He was merely burying his feelings so he didn't have to face up to them. Losing Heather should have been the worst thing that had ever happened to him, but he couldn't pretend that he felt devastated by her decision. Thinking back, perhaps he'd sensed for a while that there'd been something missing from their relationship, but he had dismissed his fears as a last-minute attack of nerves. Now he was glad that Heather had saved them both from making a terrible mistake, although it was going to be difficult to convince everyone else that was how he felt.

His friends and family would think he was putting on a brave face if he told them the truth and that would make the situation worse. He was already in line for a lot of well-meaning sympathy and he didn't intend to portray himself as the victim when he was sure that Heather had done the right thing. It might be easier if he didn't say too much and simply let people believe what they liked.

Ross felt a little easier once he had decided how to proceed. As soon as he was dressed, he went downstairs and made himself a pot of coffee. He telephoned his mother while it was brewing, but there was no reply. She'd told him that she was going to have her hair done that morning and he could only assume that she wasn't back yet.

He phoned the vicar instead and explained what had happened, politely refusing the man's well-meaning offer of counselling. There was no danger of him falling apart— that just wasn't his way. He would cope perfectly well with what had happened so long as the people around him let him do it his way. He knew what he wanted from life and he refused to let this setback alter his plans. He had worked too hard to prove himself to give up his dreams now.

Fired up by the same determination that had driven him all his adult life, Ross carried on making calls. He had just finished speaking to the florist when the doorbell rang and he went to answer it, unsurprised when he found Ben Nicholls, his best man, on the step. Ben grinned as he followed him inside.

'So how do you feel this morning? Ready to face your fate, I hope.'

Ross shrugged as he headed back to the kitchen and poured Ben a cup of coffee. 'There's been a change of plans. The wedding has been called off.'

'Oh, ha-ha, very funny. If you think I'm going to fall for that, you can think again.' Ben plonked himself on a chair and gulped down a mouthful of coffee. 'Oh boy, I needed that! Would you believe that I got called into work last night? Some idiot on a motorbike decided to play chase with a police car and hit a bollard in the process. He was in a right mess, I can tell you.'

Ross didn't interrupt as Ben regaled him with the tale

of the injured motorcyclist. They often exchanged stories about their working lives. As a GP in a busy town-centre practice, Ross was used to dealing with all kinds of medical matters ranging from the mundane to the life-threatening. He enjoyed the orderliness of general practice work, though, and wouldn't have traded it for the adrenaline rush that Ben got from working in the emergency department at the local hospital.

He waited until Ben ran out of steam then returned the conversation to the subject uppermost on his mind. 'Actually, I wasn't joking. Heather sent me a letter last night to say that she'd changed her mind. The wedding has been called off.'

'You're not serious, are you?' Ben demanded, gaping at him.

''Fraid so.' Ross gave his friend a tight smile, hoping the news wouldn't trigger a sudden outpouring of sympathy. He neither deserved nor wanted to be on the receiving end, quite frankly. 'It means that I'm going to need your help to sort things out.'

'Of course. It goes without saying that I'll do anything I can,' Ben said quickly. He sat up and stared at Ross. 'Did Heather say why she'd changed her mind? I mean, there isn't someone else involved, is there…?'

Ben tailed off, obviously unsure what to say now that he had voiced the question, and Ross sighed. He suspected it was a question he would have to get used to answering in the coming days.

'Not as far as I'm aware. Heather simply wrote that she'd realised it would be a mistake if we got married.'

'And that was it? You didn't go to see her and talk it all through?'

'No. She'd made her position perfectly clear in her letter.'

'Fair enough.'

It was obvious that Ben thought he'd been wrong to have left it there. Ross frowned, wondering if he should have gone to see Heather and pressed her for an explanation. Had she met someone else, as Ben had suggested, someone she loved more than him?

He tested out that theory, unsure what his reaction would be if it proved to be true, but he felt very little. He certainly didn't feel jealous at the thought of her seeing another man and that was something else he needed to think about later. If he didn't feel jealous or even very upset then why had he asked Heather to marry him in the first place? Because she had ticked all the right boxes and fitted his ideal of the perfect wife?

It was alarming to realise how calculating he'd been. Ross cleared his throat, not sure that he liked discovering something so negative about himself. 'Anyhow, I've phoned the vicar and told him. I've also been on to the florist and cancelled the flowers. I still need to contact the car-hire firm and the hotel where the reception was being held. Fortunately, we decided not to go away on honeymoon until the spring, so that's one less job to deal with. But I did book the bridal suite, if you remember, so that will need to be cancelled too.'

'I can do all that for you,' Ben offered immediately.

'Thanks.' Ross gave him the phone numbers then found the guest list that Heather had tacked to the bulletin board next to the fridge. 'I need to go and see my mother, and let her know what's happened, so if you could make a start on phoning the guests as well, I'd be really grateful.'

'No problemo.' Ben took the list from him, grimacing when he saw the number of people who had been invited. 'I don't imagine we'll be able to get hold of everyone before they set off, so d'you want me to go to the church and meet them there?'

'I'm not sure. It might be better coming from me.' He shrugged when Ben looked at him in surprise. 'Some of those people are travelling quite a distance and it seems a bit rich to turn them away at the door. I'd feel better if I did it myself.'

'Well, if you're sure you're up to it…'

'It isn't a problem,' Ross assured him briskly, not wanting to admit how indifferent he felt about the idea. This should have been his worst nightmare, yet he felt unmoved by the prospect of cancelling all the arrangements. How odd.

Once again he shied away from examining his feelings too deeply. Standing up, he reached for his car keys. 'I'll leave it with you, then. I'll get over to Mum's and break the news to her before the grapevine gets to work. Give me a call if you have any problems. I've got my phone with me.'

'Will do. And, Ross, I'm really sorry about what's happened.'

'Thanks. Although it's probably better that it happened now rather than later,' Ross said bluntly, heading for the door.

He left the house and got into his car. It was the second week of December and the weather was very cold. The forecast had predicted a dry sunny day—perfect for a wedding at this time of year. As he drove through the town, Ross tried to imagine how the day might have gone, but it was impossible to picture it. It was as though all the months of preparation had never happened, as though there never had been a wedding about to take place that day, *his* wedding.

In a sudden rush of insight he realised that he had merely gone through the motions, done what had been expected of him, but he had never connected emotionally with the event. Getting married had been just another step on his life plan, another box that had needed ticking. Was it any wonder that Heather had changed her mind about marrying him?

There was an envelope lying on the mat when Gemma Craven went downstairs on Saturday morning. She frowned as she picked it up. The post usually didn't arrive until lunchtime, so it was a surprise to see it lying there at this hour of the day.

Her frown deepened when she turned the envelope over and discovered that there was no stamp or address on it, just her name. Ripping open the flap, she took out the single sheet of paper it contained, feeling her heart leap into her throat as she tried to make sense of what it said. It was from Heather, telling her that the wedding had been called off.

Gemma sank down onto the stairs in a state of shock. Was it true? Had Heather really decided not to marry Ross? She couldn't imagine why her friend would have done such a thing, but there was no doubt that the signature on the bottom of the letter was Heather's. What on earth had happened to make Heather do such a thing?

Scrambling to her feet, she hurried to the phone and dialled Heather's home number, but there was no answer even though she let it ring a dozen times. She tried her friend's mobile phone next but the call went straight through to voice mail. She left a brief message, letting Heather know she was worried about her and asking her to call back, and hung up. She wasn't sure what she should do now. The arrangement had been that she would go round to Heather's home to help her get ready. As the chief and only bridesmaid, Gemma's job was to attend to the bride, but if there was no wedding then her services were no longer needed. However, she couldn't sit at home, wondering what had happened. She had to find out what had gone on, and why Heather had decided not to marry Ross.

Gemma's heart lurched as a picture of Ross Mackenzie suddenly appeared in her mind's eye. The saying about tall, dark and handsome could have been coined for him. At a little over six feet in height, Ross was tall enough to stand out in a crowd and that was before you added in all the rest. With his black hair and cobalt-blue eyes, he drew admiring glances wherever he went. His features were both attractive and very masculine—a strong chin, chiselled lips, a straight nose. He played tennis in the summer and skied in the winter and his body definitely bore testament to the benefits of all that exercise. His whole bearing was that of a man in command of his life. Ross knew what he wanted and he got it, too. He'd wanted Heather to be his wife so what had gone wrong?

Gemma ran back upstairs to her bedroom. Scooping up the armful of clean clothes she'd left over the back of a chair the night before, she hurried into the bathroom. She couldn't explain the urgency she felt to see Heather. All she knew was that she had to make her friend understand what a mistake she was making. Most women would give their right arm to marry Ross, yet Heather had thrown away her chance of happiness.

Ten minutes later Gemma left the house, shivering as the chill of a frosty December morning hit her. She hurried to her car, groaning when she discovered the windscreen was covered with ice. She wasted another couple of minutes clearing it away and her fingers were frozen solid by then, the tips of them turning pink with cold.

She slid into the driving seat, cranking up the heater to its highest setting, not that there was much hope of any warmth just yet. Still, at least it provided her with the illusion that she might soon start to defrost, although maybe the chill she felt didn't stem solely from the weather. It was the thought of how upset Ross must be that was making her feel so cold. He must be devastated—completely devastated!

Gemma's breath caught on a sob but she forced it down as she headed towards the centre of Dalverston. Heather lived with her father on the far side of the town and Gemma had to brave the traffic to get there. Normally, at this time on a Saturday morning the roads would have been fairly clear, but with Christmas a couple of weeks away, there was already a build-up of cars and that delayed her. By the time she reached the house, she was so tense that she was trembling. She parked in the drive then hurried to the front door and rang the bell. Matthew Thompson, Heather's father, greeted her with a weary smile.

'I take it that Heather's told you she's called off the wedding?'

'She pushed a note through my door. I found it on the mat this morning when I got up.'

Gemma followed him into the house, shivering appreciatively as a blast of warm air hit her. Matthew led the way to the kitchen, obviously expecting her to follow him. Picking up the teapot, he offered it to her and she nodded.

'Please.'

He poured them both a cup of tea and placed them on the table by the window. Gemma frowned when she saw that his hands were shaking. Heather's decision to cancel her wedding must have been a shock for her father too.

'Did Heather say why she's decided not to marry Ross?' Gemma asked as they sat down.

'No. She just said that she'd realised it would be a mistake.'

Matt's whole bearing seemed to have altered overnight; he appeared years older that morning. It was upsetting to see him looking this way when Gemma had always thought how full of life he usually was. He ran the busy general practice where she worked as one of the practice nurses with the vigour of a man half his age, but he looked grey and gaunt as he sat there, sipping his tea.

'Is Heather here?' she asked gently, not wanting to add to his distress by pressing him for answers.

'No. She left last night, caught the last train to London, in fact.' Pain darkened his eyes. 'I should have realised she had doubts about getting married and made sure it was what she really wanted instead of adding to the pressure she felt to go along with it.'

Gemma looked at him in surprise. 'It was Heather's decision to marry Ross. Nobody pushed her into it.'

'Maybe.' Matthew gave her a grim smile then looked round when the doorbell rang. 'Excuse me. I'd better see who that is.'

Gemma drank some of her tea after he left the kitchen. It seemed her trip had been a waste of time if Heather wasn't here. She had no idea what she should do now, or if there was anything she *could* do. Going to see Ross was out of the question, of course. He would be far too upset to see her.

The sound of voices made her glance round and she felt her heart leap when she saw the two men coming along the hall. Matthew was tall but the man with him topped him by a couple of inches. In the wintry light filtering through the kitchen window, his skin gleamed like burnished gold, the perfect foil for his startling bluer-than-blue eyes.

Gemma felt a shudder run down her spine, then another until it felt as though her whole body was quaking. She had tried so hard to ignore these feelings, tried and, to some extent, succeeded too. Every time she'd found herself reacting to the sight of him, she'd reminded herself of all the reasons why it was wrong: he was her best friend's fiancé; he wasn't interested in her; he definitely wouldn't find her attractive—especially if he saw her naked.

All those points still held good. Maybe the first one was in doubt but weddings had been called off and rescheduled before, and there was no saying this one wouldn't be either. However, the second two points were as valid now as they had always been. Ross wasn't interested in her and he most definitely wouldn't find her attractive in bed. No man in his right mind would.

Gemma knew there was no hope wishing she could have a chance to win Ross's love, but that didn't stop the tingles, the shivers, the mini-earthquakes that were assailing her as he came into the room. Her head understood the truth, but her heart was deaf, dumb and blind to it, steadfastly believing that if she loved Ross enough from afar, one day he might learn to love her in return.

CHAPTER TWO

Ross ground to a halt when he spotted Gemma sitting at the table. He hadn't realised there was anyone else in the house and for a moment he was tempted to beat a hasty retreat. However, he would have to face people at some point and there was no time like the present.

'Gemma.'

He nodded politely to her, seeing the wash of colour that ran up her face. With that silver-blonde hair and flawless porcelain skin, she must find it difficult to hide her feelings, he thought, then wondered why the idea had occurred to him now of all times. He had worked with Gemma for almost three years, ever since she had moved to Dalverston to take up the post of senior practice nurse at the surgery. She and Heather had soon struck up a friendship, so there had been many occasions when they had met outside work, too. However, he had never even noticed her hair or her skin before. How strange.

He turned away, uncomfortable with the way he was behaving. Maybe it had been a shock to be dumped if not literally at the altar but pretty close to it, but did that really explain why his mind seemed to be whizzing off at tangents all of a sudden?

'Ross, I don't know what to say apart from the fact that I'm really and truly sorry.'

Ross cleared his mind of all extraneous thoughts when he heard the pain in Matthew's voice. 'If Heather had any doubts then she was right to call off the wedding,' he said quietly, not wanting to add to the older man's distress. 'It would have been much worse if she'd gone ahead and regretted it later.'

'That's what Heather said.' Matt sank down onto a chair as though he was too weary to remain standing. He waved Ross to a seat. 'Sit down. Would you like some tea? There's some made…'

He went to get up again but Gemma quickly intervened. 'I'll get it.'

She stood up, easing around Ross with a murmured 'Excuse me'. Ross felt a ripple of awareness run through him as she brushed against him in passing, and frowned. How many times had that happened over the last three years? There must have been dozens of occasions when he and Gemma had touched and he'd barely registered it, yet all of a sudden his brain was flashing signals along his nerves, alerting all the muscles and sinews to the fact that there was a young and attractive female in close proximity. And when he thought *all* his muscles, he meant all too.

He hurriedly sat down, stunned by what was happening to him. All right, so he was a normal healthy male with a normal healthy male's interest in the opposite sex. However, was it really *normal* to be experiencing these feelings on the morning of what should have been his last day of bachelorhood?

Confusion clouded his mind so that when Gemma put a cup of tea in front of him he couldn't even thank her. He took a gulp of the tea in the hope that it would ease the kinks out of his system. Maybe he needed to face up to his feelings instead of bottling them up? After all, he'd been looking forward to building a life with Heather, and to have his plans scuppered was bound to have hit him hard. Although he did feel a certain sense of relief, underneath that surely he was both upset and hurt?

Ross felt a little twinge deep inside him, not quite pain but something similar, and breathed a little easier. Of course he was upset and, that being the case, it was understandable if he was behaving oddly. He dredged up a smile, forcing his body to downgrade the alert from red to amber.

'I take it that Heather isn't here?' he said, addressing himself to Matthew. He was aware in one part of his mind that Gemma had gone to refill Matt's cup but he didn't dwell on it. It had no relevance whatsoever to what had happened.

'No. She left last night, caught the last train to London.' Matt looked at him in despair. 'I don't know what she's going to do there. I mean, she doesn't know anyone and she has nowhere to live. London's a big place. Heaven only knows what could happen to a woman on her own…'

His voice broke and he stared down at the table, overcome by fear for his daughter. Ross wished he could think of something to say, but anything he came up with sounded trite. It was left to Gemma to intervene again. Walking around the table, she laid a gentle hand on Matt's shoulder.

'Heather will be fine. You mustn't worry about her. She's bright, resourceful and more than capable of looking after herself.'

She smiled at the older man, a smile of such compassion that Ross felt his heart ache with longing. All of a sudden he longed for some of that compassion for himself. He wanted Gemma to smile at *him* and make him feel that everything would be fine and that someone cared. That *she* cared. The thought startled him so much that he flinched, but thankfully the other two didn't notice.

'You really think so?' Matt asked desperately and Gemma nodded, her silky pale hair falling over her cheek for a moment before she tucked it behind her ear.

'Yes, I do. You did a really great job of raising her, Matt, and she isn't going to go off the rails just because she's moved to the city.'

Another smile, another gentle squeeze of the shoulder before she moved away; however, Ross's eyes remained locked on her. He didn't *want* to watch her but he couldn't stop himself. She picked up the cup and brought it back to the table, and once again her hair fell softly over her face as she bent and placed it in front of Matt. Ross felt his breath catch in anticipation as he waited for her to do it again, tuck that silky, satiny lock of hair behind her ear…

His whole body went into spasm as he watched her anchor it back into place. Now he could see the delicate curl of her ear, see how small and pale it looked, almost translucent, like a shell that had been washed clean by the sea. Ears had been just ears to him before. He understood their structure and could have explained in simple terms why they were necessary. However, Gemma's ear—so delicate, so beautiful—was more like a work of art than an anatomical fact. He could have sat there and studied it all day!

* * *

Gemma sat down at the table, carefully keeping her eyes on her cup. Ross was staring at her and she couldn't for the life of her understand why. She took a sip of her tea then almost choked as a thought occurred to her: did Ross believe that she'd known Heather had been planning to call off the wedding?

'I had no idea what Heather was going to do.' She turned to him in dismay. The worst thing was that she actually *felt* guilty even though she'd had no idea what her friend had been planning. As far as she'd been aware, Heather had been madly in love with Ross, and he with her.

The thought stung and she rushed on when he failed to answer. 'It's true, Ross. I swear, I didn't know that Heather was going to call off the wedding.'

'It doesn't matter.' He made a visible effort to collect himself. Picking up his cup, he swallowed some of the tepid tea and grimaced. If there was one thing he loathed it was lukewarm tea.

'Of course it matters,' Gemma snapped, suddenly angry with him. The least he could do was to be honest. Surely she warranted that much respect? She almost snatched the cup out of his hand and stood up. 'Heather didn't tell me, so if you've got it into your head that I knew something was wrong but was holding out on you, you can forget it.'

'As I said, it doesn't matter.'

There was an answering bite in his voice which was so out of character that Gemma did a double take. He gave her a tight smile, his blue eyes as bright and as cold as sapphires as he stared at her, and she was more convinced than ever that he did believe she'd had a hand in her friend's decision. 'The deed's done, Gemma, so who knew what and when isn't relevant. What's important now is that we sort things out with the minimum of distress for everyone concerned.'

He held her gaze, daring her to proclaim her innocence a third time, but she wasn't that foolish. Heads connecting with brick walls was a concept she had no intention of investigating at first hand. She smiled sweetly at him, her grey eyes as chilly as she could make them.

'Of course. And it goes without saying that I'll help any way I can.'

'Thanks, but it's all covered.'

He brushed aside her offer of help and Gemma's mouth compressed. Ross may be every woman's dream but he could also be her worst nightmare when he got into one of his stubborn moods. He was so focussed that once he got an idea into his head, it was impossible to shift it.

The thought was less than reassuring. Spinning round, she marched to the counter and switched on the kettle to make a fresh pot of tea. She needed to keep busy and could do with another cup to settle her nerves. As for Ross, well, she really didn't care if he wanted tea or anything else. No wonder Heather had dumped him. He was so bloody arrogant, so opinionated, so…so…

Gorgeous, an inner voice suggested before she squashed it. As her grandmother had been fond of saying, handsome is as handsome does. She must remember that the next time she got the collywobbles around Dr Always-Right Mackenzie!

Gemma was still thinking evil thoughts and enjoying them too when the phone rang. Matthew sighed as he got up. 'I expect this will be the first of many once the news gets out.'

There seemed little anyone could say to that so Gemma stayed silent, pouring the boiling water into the pot and popping on the lid. Ross seemed equally disinclined to talk, so she sat down and stared into space while the tea brewed, wondering if she should leave as soon as Matt came back. Ross had made it clear that her help wasn't needed...

'I'm sorry. I don't know why I said that. I seem to be all over the place this morning.'

Her gaze flew to him when he spoke and her heart, not to mention her anger, melted when she saw the bewilderment in his eyes. Ross was always so centred that it was a shock to see him looking this lost. Impulsively, she reached over and squeezed his hand.

'And I'm sorry, too, for being so snappy. I had no right. After all, it's you who's suffering. This must be terrible for you, Ross.'

All of a sudden her eyes filled with tears and she heard him sigh. 'Don't upset yourself on my account, Gemma. I'm fine—really, I am.'

'How can you be?' She dug a tissue out of her pocket and blew her nose. 'You must be in a state of shock—I am. I mean, I love Heather to bits. She's the best friend anyone could have, but I can't understand why she's done this— and to you of all people.'

She hurried on when she saw his brows rise as he caught the vehemence in her tone. The last thing Ross needed at the moment was her admitting how she felt about him... Correction: the last thing Ross needed was her admitting how she felt about him, *ever*.

'You two are perfect for each other. You have so much in common between your work and the things you enjoy doing. If I'd had to pick the ideal partner for either of you then I would have chosen Heather for you and you for Heather.'

'That's what I thought. Heather was perfect. She ticked all the right boxes.' He broke off, looking a little embarrassed, and Gemma hastened to assure him there was no need.

'And that's why you fell head over heels in love with her,' she said encouragingly.

'Ye-e-s-s.'

There was something in his voice that made her stare at him. Had that been a hint of doubt she'd heard? Was Ross not sure—not one hundred and ten per cent sure—that he loved Heather with his whole heart? The thought was intriguing but before she could pursue it, Matt returned, looking more grim-faced than ever.

'That was Ambulance Control on the phone. There's been an incident on the canal, along that stretch which is being refurbished about ten miles south of here. One of the cranes has collapsed and there's at least a dozen people injured, apparently.'

'Have they despatched the rapid-response team?' Ross demanded, standing up.

'Yes, but there's a snag. It appears there's some sort of a problem with the fuel they use for the ambulances and other emergency vehicles. The whole fleet is off the road, apart from one paramedic car.' Matt grimaced. 'Ambulance Control has called for assistance from the neighbouring authorities but it's going to be a while before they can get any ambulances here.'

'And in the meantime they want us to do whatever we can,' Ross guessed.

'Exactly. I know it's the worst possible day for something like this to happen, but we don't have a choice, do we?'

'No.' Ross headed for the door. 'I'll get straight over there and see what I can do. Ben's at my house, luckily enough, so I'll pick him up en route.'

'That would be a real help. I'll phone Rachel and the others and follow you down.' Matt turned to Gemma. 'We're going to need all the help we can get from the sound of it, Gemma, so can we count you in?'

'Of course.' Gemma jumped to her feet and hurried to the door.

'Why don't you come with me?' Ross suggested as they all trooped into the hall. He paused, forcing Gemma to stop to avoid bumping into him. 'That stretch of the canal is quite difficult to reach. The fewer vehicles that are there, blocking the way, the better.'

'That's a point,' Matt concurred. 'Heaven knows what sort of machinery they'll need to shift that crane but there's no point cluttering up the area. I'll pick up Rachel and the others and that will help to keep the number of vehicles to a minimum.'

It was all sorted out without Gemma saying a word, not that she could have objected to going with Ross—that would have been too difficult to explain. She could hardly have admitted that the thought of being in the car with him was giving her hot and cold chills.

She slid into the rear seat, murmuring something about leaving the front passenger seat free for Ben. Ross obviously saw nothing strange in that, but he had no reason to be suspicious. He didn't know that the thought of sitting next to him would have been torture for her. To feel his shoulder brush against hers, to smell the scent of his skin, to absorb the powerful force of his masculinity would have been both heaven and hell, and she couldn't handle it. Not today. Not *this* day when he should have been on his way to church to marry her best friend.

She needed time to gather her thoughts and return them to the box mentally marked 'Forbidden' where they had resided for the last three years. Only then would she be able to cope, when Ross was back in his rightful place as her best friend's fiancé… Only he was no longer that, was he? He was neither engaged to Heather nor married to her. To all intents and purposes, he was a free agent now. Available. Obtainable. Although not for someone like her. Not for a woman whose body had made men recoil in revulsion.

Pain speared through her heart as she stared out of the car window. *She* could only *ever* love Ross from afar.

CHAPTER THREE

GEMMA had been seventeen when her whole life had changed. She had been in her first year at sixth-form college and just finding her feet as an adult. She had been enjoying her studies and enjoying the new opportunities to socialise. Life had been exciting, exhilarating, fun.

When her friend Katie suggested that they go to Sheffield to see a concert, Gemma was thrilled. Katie had passed her driving test a few months earlier and the plan was that she would drive them there. Gemma pleaded with her parents to let her go and in the end, they agreed. They knew Katie and trusted her.

The concert was as good as they had hoped it would be. Gemma and Katie were on a high as they drove home afterwards, singing along to a CD of the bands they had seen that night. They were within a mile of home when a car suddenly pulled out of a side road and rammed straight into them.

Gemma took the brunt of the impact. Part of the door embedded itself into her side, slicing through her left kidney and damaging her spleen. There was extensive tissue damage, broken ribs, bruising to her spine, although, mercifully, she was unaware of how severe her injuries were. The long weeks she spent in ICU were a blank. She remembered nothing about them, although her parents told her later that twice they were warned to prepare themselves when it looked as though she was about to lose her battle to survive. Yet somehow, against all the odds, she pulled through.

Once she left Intensive Care she underwent months of physiotherapy plus more surgery. Her kidney had needed to be removed as well as her spleen, but the surgeons assured her that she would be able to function perfectly well without either organ. What they couldn't do anything about was the extensive scarring from the many operations she'd needed, but that seemed relatively unimportant compared to the fact that she was alive. With the support of her family, Gemma resumed her studies and soon discovered that the plans she'd made for a career in law no longer appealed. She decided to train as a nurse and help people like herself who had been injured.

It was during her final year in university that she started dating one of the other students. Up till then she'd been more concerned about catching up with her peer group, but when Mike Walsh asked her out, she accepted. Within a couple of weeks Gemma knew that she was falling in love, and the wonderful thing was that Mike felt the same way. She had told him about the accident, glossing over the fact that she still bore the scars from it because they hadn't seemed important; they were just part of her and that was that. Mike, however, viewed them in an entirely different light.

Gemma was stunned by his reaction the first time they slept together. Although he tried to hide it, she could tell he was repulsed by the sight of her damaged flesh. Every time they made love after that, she was aware that he averted his eyes from the left side of her body and never, ever, touched her there.

It was inevitable that their relationship would fail. Neither of them could cope with the continual stress. By the time they parted, all Gemma felt was relief that she would no longer be made to feel like a freak. However, it proved one thing to her: no man would find her attractive undressed. And that was when she made her decision to save herself a great deal of heartache by never having a physical relationship with a man again...

'I'll just fetch Ben. Is there anything you need? A coat, a sweater, gloves?' Ross frowned when he saw Gemma jump. She hadn't said a word on the drive to his house. She'd been so quiet, in fact, that he'd wondered if she had fallen asleep at one point. However, a glance in the rear-view mirror had soon dispelled that idea.

His frown deepened as he recalled the expression on her face. She'd looked so lost, so lonely, so much in pain, and he couldn't understand it... Unless she was upset about the wedding being cancelled? Gemma's ability to empathise with people was legendary in the surgery; all their patients remarked on how sympathetic she was. Now he couldn't help feeling guilty that she was suffering because of him. If he'd thought long and hard before he'd asked Heather to marry him, based the decision on his emotions rather than ticking all those wretched boxes, a lot of people might not be feeling quite so upset today.

It was galling to admit that he was at fault. Ross got out of the car without waiting to see if Gemma was going to take him up on his offer of extra clothing. He would take some stuff with him and she could choose what she wanted, he decided as he let himself into the house. Ben was just hanging up the phone—he grimaced when Ross went in.

'I've only managed to contact about half the people on this list. Most of them are already on their way here.'

'I'll phone the vicar and ask him to meet them at the church,' Ross said shortly, unhooking a waterproof jacket from the peg behind the door. He tossed it over a chair then rummaged through the stack of Wellington boots until he found a pair that should fit Gemma, then picked up a larger pair for himself plus a pair for Ben.

'I thought you were going to meet the ones who turned up,' Ben said uncertainly, eyeing the mound of clothing. 'Don't get me wrong. I understand if you've changed your mind. It's not something I'd relish doing either.'

'I'd go if I could but I'm afraid we're needed elsewhere.'

Ross felt around on the shelf and came up with several pairs of gloves which he added to the pile. The kitchen was starting to resemble a jumble sale but they'd be glad of the extra layers. It was bitterly cold outside and they would be frozen if they were outside for any length of time, Gemma in particular. All she had on was a sweatshirt and jeans—she'd catch her death.

The thought was far too worrying. Ross pushed it aside and opened the cupboard. Lifting out the spare pack of medical supplies he kept for emergencies, he placed it next to the chair.

'We are?' Ben's brows rose steeply. 'Why? What's up?'

'A crane has collapsed down by the canal and there are several people injured,' Ross explained, opening the pack to check that everything was there. Dressings, scissors, stethoscope, cannulas…what else? Ah, yes, saline, an essential in a situation like this.

He lifted out the box containing the pouches of fluid, and handed it to Ben. 'Here. Grab hold of this.'

'How come you've been asked to attend?' Ben demanded, taking the box from him.

'Because your lot aren't up to the job,' Ross quipped. He scooped up the clothes, swung the backpack over his shoulder and headed for the door.

'Cheek!' Ben loped along beside him. He reached around and opened the front door seeing as Ross's hands were full. 'Seriously, though, what's going on?'

'Apparently, there's a problem with the fuel that's been delivered to Dalverston's ambulance station. All the vehicles apart from one paramedic car are out of action.' He juggled the pairs of Wellingtons as he tried to unlock the boot of the car, dropped one, and cursed.

'I'll get that.'

All of a sudden Gemma was there, bending down to retrieve the recalcitrant boot. Ross nodded his thanks as he stowed the equipment in the car, then eased a waxed jacket out of the tangle of clothing and handed it to her.

'Thanks.' She shrugged it on, shivering as she zipped it up. Taking the box from Ben, she put it with the rest of the gear then slammed the boot lid.

'I can't believe this has happened!' Ben was muttering to himself as they climbed into the car. 'No ambulances? What on earth are they going to do for the rest of the day?'

'It could take longer than a day to sort things out,' Ross pointed out. He pulled out of the drive and turned right, heading towards the canal. 'Remember that problem they had down south last year? Dozens of cars broke down because there was something in the fuel? It took weeks to get them back on the road. They had to strip all the engines.'

'We can't be without an ambulance service for weeks!' Ben exclaimed. 'Lives will be lost.'

'They'll come up with some sort of a contingency plan,' Gemma said soothingly from the back seat.

'You're right.' Ben turned round and grinned at her. 'Of course they will. Sorry. I didn't mean to get my knickers in a twist!'

They both laughed, Ben at his own stupidity, Gemma at the joke, although Ross didn't join in. Ben and Gemma seemed very friendly all of a sudden. Far more friendly than he would have expected, although wasn't it tradition that romantic sparks should fly between the best man and the bridesmaid? Had Ben been looking forward to upholding that tradition, perhaps? Well, if that was the case, maybe it was a good job the wedding had been cancelled.

The force of that thought surprised him so much that the car swerved as he pulled a little too forcefully on the steering-wheel. 'Ice,' he said briefly to excuse his error. He glanced in the rear-view mirror, expecting Gemma to smile with her customary understanding, but she was staring straight ahead with an expression of such terror on her face that he was instantly contrite. The last thing he wanted was to scare her witless!

The rest of the journey passed without incident, mainly because Ross refused to let his mind wander again. The paramedic car had already arrived when they reached the canal so Ben went to speak to the driver. Ross unloaded their gear, piling everything on the ground next to the car.

'Help yourself to anything you need,' he told Gemma when she came to help him.

'Thanks.'

She picked up a woollen hat and pulled it on, silky tendrils of silver-gold hair peeking out from under the brim, and that funny wobbly feeling started up again in the pit of Ross's stomach. Lifting out the haversack, he swung it over his shoulder and headed towards the footpath that led to the canal.

'I'll go and see what's what,' he said tersely, determined to keep a rein on his emotions before they got him into trouble.

'I'll come with you,' she said immediately, grabbing a pair of gloves.

They climbed over the stile, followed the path through the copse then ground to a halt at the sight that met them. The whole arm of the crane, complete with a huge metal girder it had been lifting, had buckled and was straddling the canal from one bank to the other. Sections of metalwork had sheered off when it had collapsed and had rained down on the men who'd been working below. Ross could see a number of people lying on the ground and several others, including a boy of about ten, wandering about looking dazed. Turning to Gemma, he rattled out instructions.

'You check the guy nearest to us while I take a look at the crane driver. I'll check out the child first, though—I don't want him hanging around here any longer than is necessary. Do what you can but don't waste time if it doesn't look hopeful. Speed is of the essence here. Ben should be along soon so don't do anything stupid. And keep well away from the crane. That thing could collapse at any moment and I don't want you underneath it if it does.'

'It would mess up the surgery rosters,' she said, tongue in cheek.

'Too damned right it would,' he said with a half smile, afraid that she would realise that he was genuinely worried about her.

The thought shook him. Ross turned away and hurried over to the boy, feeling more confused than ever. For three years Gemma Craven had existed on the periphery of his life. He'd had no feelings for her, one way or another, yet all of a sudden he seemed to be awash with them. Why was it happening today of all days? Was it the shock of having his plans ruined that was causing him to behave this way?

It was the only explanation that made any sense. His life had been turned on its head today and all of a sudden he was seeing everything in a completely different light. It was strange that he should be so fixated on Gemma, though. She certainly didn't fit his ideal of the perfect woman, didn't tick all the right boxes...although she ticked a lot of others.

His mind slipped its leash again, haring headlong down a route he knew he would regret. Gemma was beautiful and sexy and far more feminine than any woman had a right to be. She had the most fabulous figure, gorgeous legs, hair that made his fingers tingle whenever he imagined touching it, and that was just for starters. She was also kind and sympathetic, good at her job and blessed with a sunny nature that made light of the most arduous tasks.

Tick, tick, tick. Box after box was being checked off and there was nothing he could do to stop it happening. Some were the same boxes he'd ticked for Heather, but there seemed to be even more to tick for Gemma. As he put a comforting arm around the boy's shoulders, he had to force down the feeling of panic that assailed him. For the first time in ages, he was responding instinctively and that was why he was finally seeing Gemma for what she was—a beautiful, sexy and desirable young woman. A woman he wanted.

The thought shocked him so much that Ross had to take a deep breath before he was able to speak. Turning the boy to face him, he performed a quick visual scan while he checked for injuries. Apart from a gash on his forehead, the child appeared unharmed, although he was obviously very frightened.

'My name is Ross and I'm a doctor,' Ross said gently. 'Can you tell me your name, son?'

'Jamie,' the boy whispered tremulously.

'Right then, Jamie, can you tell me if you're hurt?'

'My head hurts a lot,' he muttered. Tears suddenly welled to his eyes. 'I thought that crane was going to fall on top of me!'

Ross quickly sat Jamie down on the ground when his face turned paper white under his shock of bright red hair. 'It's OK, son. You've had a fright and that's why you're feeling a bit dizzy. Just put your head between your knees for me and you'll feel much better in a moment or two.'

He crouched down and waited until the colour came back to the boy's cheeks then checked him over. 'It doesn't look as though you've hurt yourself too badly. That gash on your forehead must be sore, though. It may need a couple of stitches, but that will be sorted out at the hospital.'

He glanced round, mentally crossing his fingers that Jamie's father wasn't amongst the severely injured. The site had been closed to the public for several months while work was being carried out, but it wouldn't be the first time a parent had allowed his child to accompany him to a job. 'I take it that you're here with your dad, so do you know where he is?'

'I didn't come with my dad,' Jamie admitted, looking guilty. 'Mum and Dad have gone Christmas shopping. My sister was supposed to look after me, but her boyfriend phoned and Becky told me to get lost and stop pestering her. I thought I'd come and have a look at the crane 'cos I've been dying to see it.'

'Ah, I see. So I take it that your mum and dad don't know you're here, then?' Ross said, rapidly filling in the gaps. He sighed when the boy shook his head. 'Right, then the first thing we need to do is let them know what's happened.'

He asked Jamie for his phone number and called his home. Jamie's parents were back from their shopping trip and frantic with worry because he'd gone missing. Ross explained what had happened and assured them that Jamie wasn't badly injured. They agreed to go straight to the hospital, so he handed the boy over to the paramedic who would take him there in the car. At least he hadn't had to break bad news to them, he thought as he watched the paramedic usher him away. The situation could have been a lot worse, although he suspected that Jamie and his sister might find that Santa wasn't quite as generous with his presents this year!

Ross hurried over to the crane and carefully climbed up into the cab. The driver was unconscious and it was immediately apparent that he was in a very bad way. He grimaced as he eased himself between the broken spurs of metal. A lack of Christmas presents was the least of this poor fellow's worries.

* * *

Gemma watched as Ross hurried over to the boy, then turned and headed towards the nearest casualty, a young man in his twenties. Kneeling down beside him, she drove all other thoughts from her mind. She wasn't going to worry about what seemed to be bugging Ross, certainly wasn't going to compromise her patient's well-being by not staying focussed. Maybe Ross had been uncharacteristically sharp with her, but he had a lot on his mind, with the wedding being cancelled, so it was understandable. She certainly mustn't go reading anything into it.

'Hi, my name is Gemma and I'm a nurse. Can you tell me your name and where it hurts?'

'Aidan Donnelly and my right arm is killing me.' The young man groaned as he tried to move his injured arm and Gemma quickly stopped him.

'Lie still. I'll check you over and do what I can. OK?'

'Fine.'

Aidan lapsed back onto the grass, groaning as she gently felt from his shoulder to his wrist. There was little doubt in her mind by the time she finished that the humerus was fractured mid-shaft. She checked his fingers next as this type of break could cause damage to the brachial artery and discovered that they felt cold to the touch and were turning blue, both worrying signs.

She quickly checked the pulse in Aidan's right wrist and her fears were confirmed when she couldn't detect one. Although the injury wasn't life-threatening, ischaemia—an inadequate blood supply—could result in long-term damage and she was anxious to prevent that happening.

She looked round when she heard voices and was

relieved when she saw Ben and the paramedic coming towards her. She went to meet them, lowering her voice so that Aidan wouldn't overhear them. 'This chap has a fractured humerus. There's no pulse in his right wrist and his fingers are cold and turning blue.'

'That needs sorting, asap,' Ben said, turning to the paramedic. 'Can you ferry him back to hospital as well, Charlie? He should be OK to travel by car once you've splinted his arm. Make sure ED knows that he requires immediate treatment. That artery needs to be freed and the blood supply restored pronto if he's to regain full use of his hand and wrist.'

'I'll go and check on the others,' Gemma said once she was sure that Aidan was being taken care of.

She told Aidan that he would be going to hospital then made her way to the next casualty, a middle-aged man. A section of metal had fallen on him, pinning him to the ground. He was lying face down, his hard hat obscuring his face. Gemma checked for a pulse at both neck and wrist but there was none. It was impossible to turn him over because of the weight of the metal, but she knew there was nothing she or anyone else could do for him. She left him there and hurried to the next person, arriving at the same time as Ben. He grinned at her as they both knelt down.

'Not quite what I'd planned on doing today.'

'Me neither,' Gemma agreed, glancing across at the crane. Ross was leaning into the cab while he attended to the driver. He seemed oblivious to the danger he was in or maybe he didn't care. Maybe his apparent calm was all a front and inside he was so devastated about losing Heather that he no longer cared what happened to him.

The thought was sheer torture. Gemma knew she couldn't cope with it if she hoped to do her job properly. She dragged her gaze away and forced herself to concentrate on the injured man. There was a lot of blood on his face and that worried her until Ben discovered that he had broken his nose. That explained the heavy bleeding and a quick examination along with a few pertinent questions—name, age, what day of the week it was—soon established that he hadn't suffered a serious head injury. He would need to be checked again when he reached hospital, of course, but she and Ben were happy to move on to the next casualty.

'I hate to interrupt but I need a hand over there.'

All of a sudden Ross was standing beside them, sounding unusually curt again as he addressed himself to Ben. Gemma felt her heart ache because it was so unlike him to speak to anyone this way. He was always totally professional in his dealings with the staff at the surgery, never lost his temper, and was always calm and reasonable. He must be devastated by what had happened to behave so out of character, and there wasn't a thing she could do about it, either.

'Typical. Gemma and I were just doing a bit of bonding and now you want to drag me away.' Ben leered at her so comically that Gemma couldn't help smiling then wished she hadn't when she saw Ross's expression darken.

'Well, I'm sorry to spoil your fun but you're the expert here. I'm just a humble GP, don't forget.'

Ben whistled softly as Ross stalked away. 'Ouch! That put me in my place, didn't it? This wedding business has hit him really hard. It's not like Ross to bite people's heads off like that. I knew it was odd this morning when he told me what had happened. I mean, he didn't even *sound* upset. He must have been bottling it all up until now.'

'Probably,' Gemma agreed sadly. 'I just wish there was something we could do.'

'To get Ross and Heather back together, you mean?' Ben's face lit up. 'Great idea! It's a crying shame, them breaking up like that. He and Heather are just perfect for each other. They're so well matched that it's disheartening, really. You just know that you'll never find anyone as perfect yourself, or, more to the point, someone who thinks you're perfect for them.' His smile dimmed. 'I certainly won't.'

Gemma had a feeling there was more to that comment than Ben was admitting. However, there was no time to ask him to explain when there were so many lives at risk. She finished attending to their patient while Ben went to help Ross, using a wad of lint to clean away the blood. By the time that was done, the police had arrived, bringing with them more members of Dalverston's rapid response team, although as one wit pointed out they might need a new name after today seeing as their response had been far from speedy.

It was good to have so many experienced people around, though. Gemma did whatever she was asked, unconcerned when at times she found herself acting as gofer. She wasn't too proud to admit that other people knew more about emergency procedures than she did and was happy to learn from them. It was different in the surgery—she was completely at home there and confident that there was little she couldn't handle, but this wasn't her natural element.

Her gaze strayed once more to Ross, who was in the thick of things, helping the team attend to the crane driver.

Even as she watched, she saw him issue instructions to one of the paramedics and saw the man obey them. No matter where Ross worked, or in what capacity, he would feel completely sure of himself. Heather had been exactly the same. No wonder they'd been so right for each other. Two good-looking, talented, perfect people who should have had a perfect life together.

Tears filled her eyes and she hurriedly turned away. She wasn't perfect and she never could be. The scars on her body might have faded but they were still there, still looked repulsive to anyone who saw them. Even if Ross and Heather never got back together, even if Ross realised that he could find someone else equally perfect for him, it wouldn't be her.

CHAPTER FOUR

'THERE'S no way we can risk lifting him out of here even on a spinal board. We'll need the air ambulance to winch him out.'

Ross sank back onto his heels, curbing the urge he felt to question Ben's decision. He wasn't sure why he felt so bloody minded. After all, his friend dealt with injuries like this every day. Normally, he would have deferred to Ben's expertise without a second thought, so what was different today? Was it pique over the way Ben and Gemma seemed to have become best buddies all of a sudden?

The thought did nothing to enhance his mood. Fortunately, another voice entered the conversation then, sparing him from having to reply. 'I'll get the police to radio back to base and request the helicopter.'

Sam Kearney, one of the newer additions to Dalverston's rapid response team, hurried off to set things in motion, giving Ross a very necessary breathing space. He took advantage of it, breathing in and out a couple of dozen times, although it didn't achieve very much. Ben and Gemma an item? No way!

'Can you help me get this collar on him?'

Ben's request interrupted his flow of thoughts. Ross eased himself a little further into the confines of the cab and supported the driver's head while Ben strapped a cervical collar around his neck. The driver, a man called Sandy Walsh according to the ID tag attached to his overall pocket, was still unconscious, but that was a blessing in the circumstances. He had suffered extensive facial injuries, including a shattered eye socket, a broken cheek bone and a fractured jaw. Several broken ribs, a suspected fractured femur and what looked like a Pott's fracture to his left ankle could all be added to the list, although Ross suspected more would be discovered once they got him to hospital.

'Thanks. With a bit of luck the air ambulance will be at Base and we won't have to wait too long.' Ben sat back and regarded Ross with concern. 'How are you holding up?'

'Fine.' Ross returned the look with one just the upper side of chilly. 'This isn't the first emergency call I've attended.'

Ben waved a dismissive hand. 'I didn't mean that. This type of situation is perfectly suited to you, Ross. In fact, I'd go so far as to say that you'd be an ideal candidate for emergency work if you wanted.'

'That's nice to know,' he replied drily, wondering where the conversation was leading. 'However, I'm quite happy with what I do so don't worry that I intend to encroach on your territory.'

'Oh, I'm not worried on that score.' Ben shrugged. 'You may be temperamentally suited to emergency work, but it's not your scene. It's too disordered for your liking. You never know what's going to happen from one minute to the next.'

'General practice isn't exactly a walk in the park,' Ross retorted, stung, and Ben held up his hands.

'I wasn't implying that it was. Sorry.' He stopped, went to speak, then stopped again. Ross sighed.

'What? I can tell you're dying to impart some pearl of wisdom, so get on with it.'

'It's you and Heather,' Ben said quickly. 'Are you sure you two can't sort this out? You guys are perfect for each other. It's a crying shame that you've split up because of some sort of stupid misunderstanding.'

'Misunderstanding?' Ross's brows rose steeply. 'Do you know something I don't? What misunderstanding are we talking about?'

'Nothing really. It's just that Gemma and I were talking earlier and we wondered if there was a way to get you and Heather back together.'

'And what did you come up with?' Ross said, his heart giving the funniest little bounce at the thought of Gemma discussing him. He hurriedly battened it down. Just because his name had cropped up in the conversation, it didn't mean anything.

'Oh, we didn't get as far as working out a plan. But maybe if you went to see Heather and told her how you felt, that you loved her, etcetera, it would help.'

Ben sounded embarrassed, as well he might, Ross thought. This wasn't the sort of conversation they'd had before. Discussing his feelings was something he avoided doing. He had learned a long time ago to keep his emotions under wraps. It made it easier to reach a balanced decision if he removed them from the equation, he'd found. Although he appreciated Ben's intentions were of the highest calibre, he could hardly explain that there was no point phoning Heather when it would mean him having to explain why. Admitting that he felt more relieved than dev-astated would lead to a lot more questions than he was prepared to answer at the moment.

'I appreciate what you're saying, Ben. Really, I do.'

'Great! So long as you'll give it some serious thought, that's the main thing.'

Ben clapped him on the shoulder to show that the touchy-feely conversation was over and everything was back to normal. Ross wished it was but in no way did anything feel normal any more. Had he ever *really* loved Heather, he wondered, the kind of love that one saw depicted in films, a love that made men weep and sacrifice their dreams?

He didn't need to think about the answer and it saddened him to know how close he had come to ruining Heather's life as well as his own. He loved Heather as a friend but now he was certain it was no more than that. He certainly wouldn't walk barefoot through hot coals for her, or forfeit his ambitions. He couldn't imagine doing that for any woman…except, possibly, Gemma.

The thought stunned him so that he found it hard to think let alone refute it. There was a roaring in his ears and he shook his head, but if anything it grew louder. Surely such thoughts about Gemma weren't affecting his hearing as well as his mind?

It was a relief when he realised that the helicopter was hovering overhead. It landed in a field beside the canal and the crew jumped out. Ross moved out of the way, leaving it to Ben and the paramedics to co-ordinate the rescue. Within a very short time the injured man was strapped to a specially adapted spinal board and winched out of the crane straight into the helicopter. The crew leapt on board and that was it. The rest of the casualties were being transported back to hospital in a variety of vehicles and now all that was left was for the accident investigators to determine what had happened. However, his role in the proceedings was at an end.

He headed over to where Ben and Gemma were standing, trying not to notice how cosy they looked together. 'That's it, then. Back to the ranch, folks?'

'Yep. Let's saddle up,' Ben quipped, earning himself another of Gemma's wonderful smiles which in its turn resulted in Ben looping an arm around her shoulders.

Ross followed them along the tow path, through the copse, over the stile, feeling like a gooseberry. It was abundantly clear to him that they didn't need his company. Tension gnawed at him as he dumped the backpack into the boot of his car then waited while the others shed their wellies. Even though it must have taken less than five minutes before they were ready to leave, he was champing at the bit and gunned the engine with a lot more verve than was necessary until he happened to glance in the rear-view mirror and saw Gemma's lips whiten.

Remorse cooled him down faster than anything else could have done. He drove them back more sedately than a maiden aunt attending a church picnic, pulling up outside his house without even the tiniest judder. Ben leapt out and opened the rear door for Gemma to alight, bowing low as she did so.

'M'lady.'

'Thank you, Nicholls,' she said with suitable hauteur. She sailed past him then stopped, eyeing the melting puddle of ice that lay directly in her path. 'And what, pray, am I supposed to do about this, my good man?'

'Apologies, m'lady.'

Ben scooped her up into his arms, ostensibly to lift her over the puddle, and Gemma smiled smugly. However, as he stepped across, he suddenly dropped her onto her feet, showering them both with icy water. Ross looked from one laughing face to the other and all of a sudden all the tensions of the day erupted.

'Oh, for heaven's sake, you two. Grow up!'

Slamming the car door, he strode up to the house and let himself in. He sighed because it wasn't their fault that he never indulged in such horseplay. He'd always taken life a little too seriously for that, always been more focussed on the important issues, like his career and his ambitions for the future.

Was that why Heather had decided not to marry him? he wondered suddenly. Had she realised that she wanted a husband who could be both a playmate and a lover? A husband who would devote as much energy to having fun as he did to achieving his goals?

Ross's heart was heavy as he walked to the sitting-room window and watched his best man and the bridesmaid having fun. Women wanted a man they could live with, laugh with, grow old with—gracefully or disgracefully, it shouldn't matter which. They wanted someone who would make them feel loved, cherished, needed, someone who wanted to be loved, cherished and needed in return, and Heather hadn't been convinced that he could fulfil either of those roles.

It wasn't Heather's fault either, but his. He'd always

held part of himself back, always been wary of giving too much in case he was rejected, and he knew why too. His reluctance to commit stemmed from the fact that his own father hadn't wanted him as a child and had rebuffed his attempts to establish a relationship with him when Ross had grown older.

His parents had never married. His mother had been just seventeen when he was born, his father a year older. Rachel, his mother, had never tried to hide the truth from him while he'd been growing up, so Ross had always known that his father hadn't wanted to play any part in his life. However, he'd clung to the fantasy that while his father might not have felt able to support a child when he'd been so young himself, it would be different when Ross was older; he'd be keen to get to know him then.

As soon as he turned eighteen, Ross set about finding him. It didn't take long because his father still lived in the same town. Ross wrote to him and asked if they could meet, and was thrilled when he received a reply almost immediately, setting up a time and a date. He was filled with anticipation as he set off that morning, sure in his own mind that this would be the start of something wonderful. He hadn't told his mother what he was doing, not because she would have tried to stop him, but because he hadn't wanted anyone to know until he'd got used to the idea himself. Having his father back in his life was such a big deal.

The man who met him in the café wasn't anything like Ross had imagined him. He looked older, sterner, his expression verging on unfriendly as he told Ross brusquely to sit down. Ross barely had time to say hello when his father informed him in no uncertain terms that Ross must never contact him again. He had his family to think about, a wife who knew nothing about the son he'd fathered by accident, children who would be hurt if they found out they had a half-brother.

By the end of the ten minutes, which was all the meeting took, Ross was in little doubt that he would never see this man again. His father didn't want anything to do with him, viewed him as a threat more than anything else. They parted after the briefest of handshakes and Ross had never tried to contact him again and he never would. He didn't need to be told twice that he wasn't wanted, but the experience had left its mark on him. He became more guarded and focussed more on his career. Although he made friends easily, attracted women by the score, he always held part of himself back. He'd never told anyone about what had happened, not his mother, not Ben, not even Heather.

He sighed as he watched Ben and Gemma laughing together. It just seemed to sum up everything that had been wrong with his and Heather's relationship. If he couldn't tell the woman he'd been about to marry something so revealing, who could he tell?

Gemma suddenly looked up and spotted him. Lifting her hand, she waved to him, her pretty face alight with laughter. Ross felt a sudden tightening in his guts, a feeling that his innards were being gripped by some force he didn't understand. Lifting his hand, he waved back, saw her face light up even more, and felt a rush of powerful emotion run through him. He could tell Gemma his secret, he realised. He could share it with her and not feel embarrassed or ashamed. She would understand; she would care. And the thought was too much, coming as it did today of all days.

Swinging round, he turned his back on temptation, closed his heart and his mind to the idea. He had ruined one woman's life and he wasn't about to ruin another's to make himself feel better!

Monday morning rolled around and Gemma knew that the surgery was going to be a hotbed of gossip that day. News of the cancelled wedding had made its way right around the town. Even old Mr Singh in the local newsagent's had asked her why it had been called off and his conversation was usually limited to the state of the weather. Ross would be showered with sympathy, and he would hate every second of it.

Carol Walters, the practice manager, was already at her desk when Gemma arrived at Dalverston Surgery. Gemma steeled herself when she saw the curiosity on the older woman's face as she went in. As the chief and only bridesmaid, she, too, would have to run the gauntlet.

'OK, so what happened?' Carol demanded eagerly.

'I've no idea. Heather just decided that she didn't want to get married and that was it.'

'Oh, come on! There has to be more to it than that. You don't just cancel a wedding on a whim.' Carol lowered her voice. 'You can tell me, Gemma. I won't repeat what you say to another soul.'

'I know that, Carol, but I honestly don't know any more than you do,' Gemma repeated. 'If something happened to make Heather change her mind, I haven't a clue what it was.'

'No wonder my ears were burning. I hope this isn't going to be the main topic of conversation around here all day long.'

Ross's voice broke into their conversation and they both guiltily swung round. Gemma felt her heart quicken at the sight of him, but that happened every day of the week so it wasn't anything special for it to happen today, not a reason for her to get unduly worried. Maybe she had spent the weekend worrying about him but it hadn't achieved anything, neither would it. All the worrying in the world wouldn't give Ross the one thing he craved: Heather and their life together.

'I'm really sorry about what happened, Ross,' Carol said quickly. 'It must have been a real shock for you.'

'It was but, as Gemma explained, Heather just changed her mind. If anyone asks you what happened, I'd be grateful if you'd tell them that, too. It might help to dispel some of the more *fanciful* ideas that are probably circulating at the moment.'

He rolled his eyes and Carol laughed. Gemma turned away as pain speared through her heart. It was typical of Ross to want to make them feel better about being caught gossiping. Even though he must be hurting like mad, he still put other people's feelings first.

She collected her morning list from the office and headed to the nurses' room. Her first patient, a local businessman who needed a cholesterol test, had already arrived so she took the blood sample she needed and placed it in an insulated container for the courier to collect at noon. And if the pain in her heart felt a little more raw than it had before, she refused to acknowledge it. Ross was out of her league, unobtainable and definitely unavailable. There was no point wishing that she might be able to make him feel better.

By the time twelve o'clock arrived Ross was desperate to escape. The veiled looks, the sympathy, the cheer-up-you'll-survive smiles were making his head hurt. The last straw was when his mother, Rachel, another of the GPs at the practice, stuck her head round the door and looked anxiously at him.

'How are you bearing up, darling? If it's too awful then take the rest of the day off. Matt and I have discussed it and we understand—really we do—if you can't bear to be here right now.'

'I'm fine.' Ross picked up the notes he'd used and bundled them together with an elastic band ready for filing.

'You don't have to put on a brave face for me, darling,' Rachel said gently, her pretty face filled with motherly concern.

'I'm not.' He sighed. 'I'm just sick and tired of people tiptoeing around me. It was almost better to hear Gemma and Carol gossiping about me first thing this morning. At least they had the grace to admit they were curious about what had happened.'

'Gemma wouldn't have said anything bad, though,' Rachel pointed out. 'She's as worried about you as we all are, Ross.'

'Is she?' The idea was intriguing enough to chase away his irritation. He rather liked the idea that Gemma was genuinely concerned about him, funnily enough.

'Of course she is.' Rachel came into the room and gave him a hug.

'It's been an awful experience for you, Ross, and no matter how brave you're being, we all know how much it must have hurt you.'

Ross groaned inwardly when he heard the wobble in his mother's voice. They'd always been close and he hated to think that he was responsible for upsetting her. He hugged her back.

'I'll survive, Mum, really I will. What I don't want is you worrying about me because there's no need. OK?'

'If you say so, darling,' she said, although he could tell that she didn't believe him.

He gave her a quick kiss on the cheek then headed to the door. The best thing he could do at the moment was to try and behave as normally as possible and hope that it would convince her he wasn't about to fall apart. 'Right, I'll take these to the office then go for lunch. See you later.'

Thankfully, Rachel didn't try to detain him so a short time later he was heading for the café at the corner of the street. He had been intending to have a sandwich there, but changed his mind when everyone stopped talking as soon as he went in. He had never seen so many guilty faces in his life!

'Ham and cheese on wholemeal bread and a cup of black coffee to go,' he replied when the assistant asked him what he wanted. He paid for his meal then left as soon as he could, barely closing the door behind him before the chatter started up again. Obviously, his wedding, or lack of one, was proving a big hit with the local gossipmongers.

He made his way to the river, needing some time on his own while he regrouped. He hated feeling so out of sorts and a few minutes' peace and quiet would be very therapeutic. At this time of the year, it was almost deserted down there, just one lone figure sitting on a bench close to the water. It was only after he'd sat down on a neighbouring bench that Ross realised with a sinking feeling in his stomach that it was Gemma. He'd had no idea she would be there, so what should he do? Get up and leave, or stay and behave as though all the recent upheaval hadn't affected him?

He frowned because it wasn't the cancellation of his wedding, per se, that was causing him so much angst, but his lack of an emotional reaction to it. He'd found himself questioning his motives and that had been extremely disquieting. There'd also been his very strange reaction to Gemma and he still hadn't worked out what was going on there.

He took a deep breath, but there was no way that he could ignore one simple yet disturbing fact: he'd spent more time thinking about Gemma than he had about his runaway bride.

CHAPTER FIVE

GEMMA glanced round to see which other hardy soul had decided to brave the weather and almost choked on her sandwich when she saw Ross sitting on a neighbouring bench. What on earth was he doing here? She had decided not to eat her lunch in the staffroom purely to avoid him. After all the recent turmoil, it had seemed wiser to keep out of his way. But now that he was here, she wasn't sure what to do. Should she pretend she hadn't seen him, or go over and speak to him?

Before she could make up her mind, he stood up. Gemma bit her lip as she watched him walk towards her bench. He stopped in front of her, his brows rising as he nodded at the empty space beside her.

'Mind if I share your bench?'

'I…um…of course not.' She scooted over to make sure he had enough room, feeling her heart race as she watched him place his sandwich and coffee-cup on the wooden slats. He glanced up and gave her a tiny smile and her racing heart whizzed into overdrive. Gemma knew that she had to say something and blurted out the first thing that came into her head. 'About this morning, Ross, I'm really sorry. I know I shouldn't have been gossiping about you, but I never meant any harm.'

'I know.' Picking up his sandwich, he peeled back the wrapper. 'My mother said that you were worried about me.'

'Oh! Did she? Well, yes, I am. We all are,' she added hastily in case he got the wrong idea or, rather, the right one. She hurried on, not wanting thoughts like that to intrude at the moment. 'We all care about you and Heather. We just want you both to be happy.'

'Who's saying that Heather isn't happy?' he said quietly.

'But she can't be! No woman is going to be happy about cancelling her wedding. It stands to reason.'

'So you think that Heather wishes she hadn't done it?'

He took the lid off his coffee and lifted the cup to his mouth. Gemma looked away, not wanting to watch while he took a sip. There was something way too seductive about the idea of watching his lips purse as he drank from the cup. It would take very little to imagine that wonderfully mobile mouth drinking from her lips…

'I don't know,' she said, blanking out the image. 'I haven't been able to get into contact with her at all so I have no idea how she's feeling. I just know how I would feel and I'd be devastated.'

'Only if the decision wasn't one you wanted to make and I don't think that applies in this case.' He put the lid back on the cup and placed it on the bench.

Gemma stared at him in dismay. 'You think that Heather changed her mind because she no longer loves you?' she asked, scarcely able to believe what she was hearing.

'Not enough to want to spend the rest of her life with me, no.'

He sounded so final that she winced. 'I don't believe that. You two are perfect for each other. Everyone says so.'

'Perfection isn't everything, as I'm discovering,' he said flatly, staring across the grey expanse of the river.

Gemma had no idea what he meant. It seemed such a strange thing to say, especially for Ross. He strove for perfection in everything he did and achieved it too. Once again the thought of her own lack of perfection taunted her but she pushed it away. They weren't discussing her but Ross and Heather, two people who were so obviously meant to be together that it was a crime to watch them ruin their lives like this.

The urge to make him understand that overcame any reticence she felt. She touched his hand, feeling the tremor that ran from her fingertips right up her arm as their skin made contact. Despite the chilly weather, Ross's hand was warm and she shuddered as some of his heat seeped into her. It was an effort to peel her fingers away once she had his attention.

'Maybe it isn't everything, but you and Heather had something special, Ross. Surely you aren't prepared to lose that?'

'So what do you suggest I do? Go after Heather and try to change her mind?'

There was a smile on his mouth when he said that but there was no matching smile in his eyes. Gemma frowned when she saw how empty they looked. Ross must be so devastated by what had happened that he had emotionally shut down.

'Yes, if that's what it takes. Don't let pride stand in your way, Ross. If I know Heather, she's probably hoping that you will call so you can sort this out.'

'You need to take off those rose-tinted spectacles and see the situation for what it is.' His tone was brisk all of a sudden. 'Heather didn't want to marry me on Saturday and she doesn't want to marry me today or any other day. She made that abundantly clear in her letter.'

'But that's crazy! You two are just so—'

'Perfect together,' he finished for her then laughed harshly. 'I used to think that, too. The fact that we had so much in common was proof that we were an ideal match. Heather ticked so many boxes that I was sure I'd found the perfect wife and future mother of my children.'

'Boxes? What boxes?' she asked, wondering if she'd overstepped the mark by asking him that. Their conversations were normally confined to pleasantries outside the surgery. They'd never had an in-depth discussion of a personal nature and maybe she'd gone too far. However, Ross didn't appear reluctant to answer.

'I made a list of points I needed to cover when I decided to get married. Things like intelligence, the ability to interact with a wide range of people in a variety of situations, physical attractiveness, etcetera.'

He said it as though everyone compiled such a list and Gemma gaped at him. 'You're joking! Nobody chooses a partner according to some sort of...*scoring* system.'

'I did. It seemed the logical solution at the time.' He gathered up his uneaten sandwich and coffee-cup, and stood up. 'No wonder Heather decided she didn't want to be my wife.'

He walked away before Gemma could reply, not that she could think of much to say when her head was reeling. She couldn't believe that he'd been telling her the truth, yet he'd sounded completely serious. Ross had asked Heather to be his wife because she'd fitted certain criteria and not because he had fallen head over heels in love with her?

She got up because it was time she went back to work, too. However, as she made her way up the path her head was still buzzing with what she had learned. Up till now she'd imagined Ross trying to come to terms with what had happened while he dealt with a broken heart, but that might not be the case. His heart wouldn't have been broken if he hadn't been madly in love with Heather. Once he got over the shock, he would find someone else, a woman he could love this time.

Just for a moment her heart soared at the thought she might be that woman before she realised how unlikely it was. If and when Ross found someone else, he would still want somebody who was perfect in every way.

Ross went straight to his room when he got back. Sitting down at his desk, he checked the schedule lying next to the computer. The second Monday in the month was the day for the weight-loss clinic. All the doctors in the practice took it in turn to supervise the sessions and it was his turn that day. He sighed. He'd never felt less like holding a clinic in his life.

He dug the list of patients who were due to attend out of his tray. Some had been coming for a while, a couple were fairly new and one was a first-timer. The usual procedure was a talk followed by a discussion. They concluded with individual check-ups when everyone was weighed. The session normally lasted just over an hour and in no way could it be considered arduous, but could he handle it? Or should he accept his mother's offer and cry off?

He stood up abruptly. Quite apart from the fact that his mother's workload was heavy enough without him adding to it, he had never backed away from anything in his life and he wasn't about to start now. Maybe he had said too much to Gemma, told her things normally he wouldn't have shared with anyone else, but so what? He was allowed the odd lapse when he'd been cast in the role of the abandoned bridegroom through no fault of his own.

His conscience twinged because if he was honest with himself he had to accept at least half of the blame for their abandoned wedding. However, he was in no mood to, metaphorically, don a hair shirt, thank you very much. He gathered up his notes and headed to the meeting room. There were a number of people already there and he nodded to them, determined to stave off any more well-meaning offers of sympathy. He'd been dumped at the altar, not been diagnosed with some kind of life-threatening disease!

He glanced round when the door opened and felt his heart lurch when he saw Gemma come in. One of the practice nurses sat in on the clinics to answer any questions the patients felt shy about asking the doctor, and it was Gemma's turn that day. Although he appreciated her help normally, he was too conscious of what had just happened to feel comfortable about her being there. Leaving his notes on the table, he went over to her.

'If you've something else to do, I can manage in here.'

'Thanks, but there's nothing pressing that needs to be done,' she said quietly, lifting a chair off the stack piled against the wall. Its back legs caught on the one beneath, causing the whole stack to wobble dangerously, and Ross hurriedly leant forward and steadied them. This close to her he could smell the scent of the shampoo she'd used that morning to wash her hair, something delicately floral and feminine that made his nostrils tingle. He could also smell the fresh air on her skin, left over from her visit to the river, and that scent was equally stimulating. The combination was having a powerful effect on him.

Ross swallowed when he felt his body quicken with desire. That it should happen here and now stunned him. He was in the surgery, with patients waiting, yet all he could think about was Gemma and how much he wanted to reach out and touch her. What the hell was going on? Was he having some sort of breakdown? Or was this just the normal reaction of a normal man to an attractive woman? Was he, for once, allowing his needs and his emotions to overrule his head?

Gemma placed the chair at the end of the nearest row and sat down. Ross seemed transfixed by his thoughts and she could only imagine how unhappy they must be. It was clear how much he was suffering and it made her see how foolish she'd been to imagine that his heart wasn't broken. Pain washed through her but she refused to let him see how upset she felt. Turning to the woman seated on her left, she smiled brightly.

'I'm glad you came along today, Sarah. I'm sure you'll benefit from these classes.'

'I hope so.' Sarah Roberts sighed as she looked around the room. An attractive brunette in her early thirties, she had a history of yo-yo dieting and was desperate to break the cycle. 'I've tried everything—weight-loss groups, counselling, even hypnotherapy, but nothing's worked. I'm fine for a couple of weeks then something happens and I end up binge eating again.'

'You aren't the only one,' Gemma assured her. 'Several of the people here today have been down the same route as you and they're making excellent progress.'

'If I could just get my eating under control, I'd be happy. So would Martin,' Sarah added wistfully. 'He's sick and tired of me banging on about my weight all the time.'

Gemma didn't say anything. She'd met Sarah's husband when Sarah had signed up for the classes and thought him rather insensitive to his wife's problems. As far as Martin Roberts was concerned, Sarah simply lacked willpower and that was why she was struggling to maintain a healthy weight. Although willpower was a very important part of the process, Gemma knew it would take more than that to solve Sarah's eating problems. She suspected that low self-esteem was behind Sarah's ongoing battle with food.

They went through the usual procedure which involved a talk about different types of diet and the value of certain foods. Everyone present had been given an individually tailored diet sheet and there was an open discussion about the difficulties of sticking to it. By the end of the session even Sarah was joining in and sounding a lot more positive.

The clinic ended shortly before three-thirty. With evening surgery due to start at four there wasn't long to get everything cleared away. Gemma was surprised when Ross started stacking chairs against the walls as it was a job she usually performed herself.

'I can manage if you need to get ready for your patients,' she told him, attempting to place a couple of chairs onto the nearest stack.

'There's nothing to do.' Ross took them from her, effortlessly lifting them onto the pile. 'I seem to have an unusually light load tonight. I suppose I have my mother to thank for that.'

'Rachel did ask Carol if she could re-jig some of your evening appointments,' Gemma admitted. She sighed when she saw him frown. 'She's only trying to help, Ross.'

'I know, but I don't need help. I'm not ill. I've been jilted. I'll survive. To be honest, I'd welcome the opportunity to keep myself busy at the moment.'

'But why push yourself when there's no need?' she protested. 'What are you trying to prove? That you don't care about what's happened?' She shook her head so that her hair drifted across her face and she pushed it back with an impatient hand. 'Nobody's going to believe that.'

'Why not? Do I look as though I'm about to fall apart?' he demanded, but Gemma refused to back down. No matter how much he protested, she knew he was hurting.

'No, you don't. But this has still been a shock for you and no matter how hard you try to make out that you don't give a damn, nobody is going to believe it.'

'Including you?'

'Including me.' Her tone softened when she saw the uncertainty in his eyes. It was rare for Ross to project anything other than supreme confidence, and it only seemed to prove she was right. He was hurting, and hurting a lot from the look of him.

'Give yourself a break, Ross,' she continued, battening down the pain that thought aroused. 'Admit that this has knocked you for six and accept that people want to help you.'

'Is that what you want to do, Gemma—help me?'

His voice was very deep all of a sudden. It stroked along her raw nerves like a velvet-covered hand and she shivered. Her eyes rose to his as she wondered how she was going to keep her feelings hidden if he spoke to her that way. Ross was unfailingly courteous whenever he addressed her in the surgery, but he sounded so different now, and she was afraid that she might not be able to keep control of her emotions. It was only the thought of making a fool of herself that steadied her, in fact.

'Yes, of course I do. I know I'm Heather's friend, but I hope that I'm your friend, too.'

'And friends look out for one another.'

'Yes.'

Gemma wasn't sure what else she could say. She *did* want to be his friend, wanted it so much that the need was like a physical ache inside her. If they could never be anything else, then friends would have to suffice.

'Thank you.' He touched her cheek, just lightly with the very tips of his fingers, but she had to stifle her gasp. It was the first time he had consciously touched her and there was no point pretending it hadn't affected her.

She turned away, terrified that he would see how much it meant to her. 'You're welcome. Right, seeing as you're making a first-rate job of stacking those chairs, how about I make us both a cup of tea before the hordes arrive?'

'Only if there's some chocolate biscuits to go with it.'

Ross swung another couple of chairs onto the stack. Gemma gulped when she saw the muscles in his shoulders ripple beneath his shirt. It was rare that he shed his jacket at work so it wasn't as though she'd had much opportunity to get used to the sight, she excused herself as nerve endings began to hum in appreciation. She took a quick breath, forcing herself to focus on the conversation.

'D'you think it's wise to indulge in chocolate biscuits hard on the heels of the weight-loss clinic?'

'Are you saying I need to watch my weight?' he demanded, placing his hands on his narrow hips and pretending to glare at her.

'I…um…' Gemma wasn't sure what flustered her most, the sight of Ross standing there, looking so gloriously, deliciously male, or the fact that he was *teasing* her. Whichever it was, she found it impossible to string two words together and had to settle for shaking her head.

'Good. I'd hate it if we fell out so soon after we'd made friends.' He gave her a quick smile then turned back to his self-appointed task, affording her much-needed breathing space. 'As for the chocolate biscuits, well, if I can't indulge myself at the moment, when can I? I think I deserve a bit of TLC right now, don't you?'

'I do.' This time Gemma managed to force out the words. She even managed to smile when he glanced round. 'I'll go and put the kettle on.'

She quickly made her escape, hurrying along the corridor to the kitchen. Rachel and Matthew hadn't arrived yet for evening surgery, but Fraser Kennedy, their new locum, was in his room. She nodded to him as she passed but didn't stop. Although she liked Fraser, she had a more pressing task to attend to. Making Ross a cup of tea might not be the most important thing she'd ever had to do, but it marked a turning point.

He had accepted her as his friend, someone he could trust, and that meant a lot to her, although she wasn't going

to be silly enough to read too much into it. He still loved
Heather and she knew that, so she wasn't going to let
herself dream about what might have happened if her body
hadn't been so damaged. She would settle for what she
had—tea and biscuits in the staffroom with the man she
loved.

CHAPTER SIX

THE kettle had boiled by the time Ross arrived at the staff-room. He paused in the doorway and watched as Gemma poured the water into the pot. She had her back to him so he was able to study her at his leisure for once.

A wave of tenderness washed over him when he saw how focussed she was on the task. Whatever Gemma did, she gave it one hundred per cent concentration. Although Pam Whiteside, the other practice nurse, was highly efficient, Gemma had the edge. She possessed the rare ability to be both practical and sympathetic. She was also remarkably quick to recognise when a patient wasn't being completely truthful, too. There'd been several occasions, now that he thought about it, when it had been Gemma's gentle probing that had unearthed some snippet of information that had aided his diagnosis. That she carried out her duties with calm professionalism was something else he appreciated. In fact, during the three years they had worked together, he had never once seen her looking flustered until that morning.

A frown furrowed his brow as he studied her bent head. What had been wrong with her earlier? He'd had the distinct impression that she had been very on edge and he had no idea why. Was it something he'd said, or something he'd done, perhaps? He sighed because it was upsetting to think that he may have made Gemma feel uncomfortable in any way.

Thankfully, she glanced round just then and spotted him so he was able to push the thought aside. She nodded to the table which held a plate piled high with chocolate digestive biscuits. 'The biccies are all there so sit yourself down while I pour the tea.'

'Thanks.' Ross pulled out a chair, opting for the seat nearest to the plate. Gemma chuckled as she brought over their mugs and set them down.

'Don't worry. There's plenty more in the cupboard if you finish that little lot. Carol must have stocked up.'

'That's good to know.'

Ross reached for a biscuit at the same moment as she went to take one and flinched when their hands touched. He forced himself to smile, not wanting her to guess that the contact was doing serious damage to his self-control. He had managed to reason away the thought he'd had about Gemma during the clinic session because it was inappropriate to be lusting after her during working hours, and because it was out of the question for him to get involved with anyone at the moment. However, one touch of her hand and his body was revving itself up again. Surely he wasn't so desperate for sex that every woman he met was fair game?

'After you,' he said gallantly while he digested that idea. He and Heather had slept together after they had become engaged, but their sex life hadn't been either wildly passionate or very frequent. They'd both led busy lives and had agreed that spending the night together should be an occasional rather than a usual occurrence.

Was that normal? he wondered. Did engaged couples *ration* their love-making to fit in with other commitments? He had no idea, neither did he feel it was something he could ask anyone else about, certainly not Gemma. That would be a step beyond the bounds of friendship.

'Hurry up. If you're not careful, I'll have finished the whole lot while you're daydreaming.'

Ross came back to earth with a thump. 'Not a chance.' He helped himself to three biscuits and stacked them up beside his cup.

Gemma chuckled as she bit into her biscuit. 'Not taking any chances, I see.'

'Not when there's an admitted biscuit monster sitting opposite me,' he retorted, biting his biscuit in half.

'Cheek! After I've gone to the trouble of making the tea and finding the biscuits, you now think you can insult me.' She finished her biscuit and reached for another, laughing as he swatted her hand away from the plate. 'I told you there were more in the cupboard.'

'That might very well be true. But there again it might be a ploy. You could be spinning me a line so I don't panic.'

'You panic?' she scoffed. 'You have to have nerves to panic and you don't possess any, Ross Mackenzie.'

'I do. I just prefer to keep my feelings under wraps so that's why it appears that I have a heart of steel,' he said, making a joke out of the admission because he still felt wary about opening up. He'd been badly hurt by his father's rejection but deep down he knew that it was time he got over it. If he never took the risk of getting hurt then he would never know how it felt to feel great happiness either. He wanted that dream life so much—a loving wife, kids who adored him, a future filled with love and laughter. It was that thought which spurred him on.

'I've realised in the last couple of days that I need to loosen up and be a bit more forthcoming about how I feel.'

'Because of Heather?'

He heard the concern in Gemma's voice and his heart filled with warmth when he realised it was for him. 'Yes. I don't think I was very fair to her. I held too much of myself back and I'm sure that's why she decided she couldn't marry me.'

'But if you're a bit more open about your feelings, Heather might change her mind,' Gemma suggested wistfully, so wistfully that he didn't like to correct her.

It obviously meant a lot to Gemma that he and Heather should try again to make their relationship work, although he knew that nothing he did would resurrect it. To be perfectly honest, he didn't want to try. Heather may have seemed like his ideal life partner at one time, but his perceptions had changed. He was no longer sure that he and Heather would have been happy together.

It was scary to know that he'd almost made such a huge mistake and that was another incentive not to say too much. Although he was determined to make some changes to his attitude to life, he needed to take baby steps at first, not giant strides. He shrugged, leaving Gemma to draw her own conclusions, which she did.

'I'm glad, Ross. If there's anything I can do to help then just tell me, won't you?'

He almost caved in and told her the truth at that point. It was all he could do not to confess that his plan wasn't to win Heather back but to lay the groundwork for any future relationship, only it was too difficult to explain it. Gemma might think he was totally uncaring if he admitted that he'd made a mistake about Heather and that was the last thing he wanted. For some reason he couldn't explain, he couldn't bear to imagine that Gemma thought badly of him.

'Thanks. I appreciate the offer.'

'I'm sure it won't be the only one,' she assured him. 'Everyone wants to help any way they can.'

Ross's heart sank at that. Although he knew that everyone meant well, he really didn't want anyone interfering. 'I'd rather they didn't. I would much prefer to sort things out myself, and in my own way.'

Gemma laughed at his rueful expression. 'It sounds as though you're in danger of overdosing on sympathy.'

'You said it. Between the patients and Mum, it feels as though I'm drowning in it. I'm dreading the weekend. Mum will expect me to go round to hers while she cheers me up.' He shook his head. 'I don't want to hurt her feelings, but I could do without being mollycoddled!'

'You can always come round to mine if you need an excuse to escape,' Gemma suggested. She gave a little shrug when she saw the surprise on his face, wishing she'd thought about what she was doing before she'd said anything. However, now that she'd issued the invitation she could hardly take it back. 'I promise I won't mollycoddle you. I'll probably tell you to buck up your ideas if you're looking miserable!'

'Thank you,' he said, chuckling. 'It will do me a lot more good than tiptoeing around me as everyone seems to be doing.'

'Then come round about ten on Saturday morning. I've not got anything planned apart from catching up with the usual housework. You'll be able to hide away for a couple of hours,' she added, wanting to be sure he understood why she'd made the offer. The fact that she would enjoy spending the time with him was just a bonus.

She hurried on, refusing to dwell on that thought. 'We can have a cup of coffee and set the world to rights. That should take your mind off everything else.'

'It will. Thanks, Gemma. It's just what I need—a bit of normality in my life.'

'Good.'

Gemma forbore to mention that coming to her house was hardly normal for him. Although Heather had visited her home many times, Ross hadn't been there before. She quickly gathered up their cups before she got cold feet. It was just something friends did, got together for coffee and a chat, no more than that.

'I won't be stepping on anyone's toes, will I?'

'Sorry?' She glanced round uncertainly, and he shrugged.

'Your boyfriend won't object if I turn up on the doorstep?'

'That's highly unlikely,' she said crisply. 'First of all I don't have a boyfriend, and secondly I wouldn't go out with someone who was so possessive that he didn't want me to have male friends.'

'Oh, right. I see.' He paused and she looked at him questioningly.

'What?'

'I was just wondering about Ben. You two seemed to be getting on really well the other day.'

'We were. Ben's great fun,' Gemma said, unsure where the conversation was leading.

'And that's it? You two aren't involved in any way?'

'Me and Ben? Of course not! As I said, he's great fun, but that's it.'

'Right. Fine.'

Ross helped himself to the last biscuit and left. Gemma finished tidying up and went to her room. She'd only just sat down when Bev Humphreys, one of their receptionists, buzzed to tell her that her first appointment was waiting in Reception.

Gemma asked Bev to send her patient in and settled down to work. And if her mind strayed several times throughout the evening to Ross, it was understandable. If there was anything she could do to help bring him and Heather back together, she would do it. She didn't believe that Heather no longer loved him. No woman who had fallen in love with Ross would fall *out* of love with him.

She sighed. She certainly wouldn't.

By the time Saturday rolled around, the gossip was starting to die down, much to Ross's relief. Although the week had been a strain, he was hopeful that his life would get back to normal soon. He still intended to make some changes to the way he behaved, but that could only be a good thing. In fact, if he was honest, he felt as though a load had been lifted off his shoulders. Heather had done the right thing by calling off their wedding.

It was ten a.m. on the dot when he drew up outside the

tiny terraced cottage where Gemma lived. He had never been there before and he took a good long look at the place as he got out of the car. One small window downstairs, one directly above, and a front door painted poppy red. The handkerchief-sized front garden wasn't big enough for a lawn but there were lots of pots dotted about, the first glossy shoots of spring bulbs poking through the soil to welcome visitors. Although Ross's house was huge by comparison, he realised that it didn't look anywhere near as welcoming as this tiny cottage did. He rapped on the door, storing up that fact for future reference. It wasn't just internal changes he needed to make to his life, but external ones too.

Gemma opened the door, smiling warmly as she invited him in. 'Come and sit by the fire. It's freezing outside today.'

She led him through the minuscule vestibule straight into her sitting room where a fire was blazing in the grate. Not for Gemma the minimal look in décor that he favoured, Ross discovered, nor the cool neutral colours so beloved of interior designers. The room was a riot of red and gold, with touches of bronze to further liven it up. The old sofa and chair were covered in red and bronze throws, the walls painted a rich, deep gold. Every surface was covered with knick-knacks—photos in mismatched frames, china ornaments that had no intrinsic value, unlike his own expensive sculptures. It was so far removed from his own home that he was stunned into silence.

'Not your taste, is it?' Gemma said cheerfully, plumping up a scarlet velvet cushion. She tossed it back onto the sofa and laughed. 'Your face is a picture, Ross!'

'No wonder. This is all so…so…' He tailed off, unable to come up with a suitable adjective.

'Messy? Tatty?'

'No.' He shook his head, letting his mind adjust to the opulence of the colours before he tried again. '*Sumptuous*. It's so warm and vibrant, so wonderfully, fabulously inviting.' He turned to Gemma and was touched to see real pleasure on her face. Obviously, his reaction had delighted her and he realised with a jolt how much he enjoyed delighting her too.

'It's like sensory overload after my own house,' he continued, struggling to get to grips with that idea. It was as though his own happiness was suddenly all bound up with Gemma's and the thought seemed to unlock his usual reserve as he cast another look around the room.

'It's gorgeous, Gemma. Really gorgeous. Just like you.'

CHAPTER SEVEN

GEMMA felt her breath catch when she realised what Ross had said. Did he really think that she was gorgeous? she wondered, her heart racing like crazy.

'Sorry. I know how daft that must have sounded.' Ross smiled wryly. 'What I really mean is that your home is a reflection of you. It projects the same kind of warmth that you do when you're dealing with any patients in the surgery.'

'Oh, I see. Thank you. It's kind of you to say so.'

Gemma turned away, afraid that he would see how disappointed she felt. She knew it was silly to have read so much into the remark, but she couldn't help it. She longed for Ross to like her, to admire her, to want her even, but it would never happen. Leaving aside the fact that he was in love with Heather, she could never have a relationship with him that involved them being anything more than friends.

The euphoria she'd felt leaked away, leaving her feeling deflated. It was an effort to pretend that everything was fine as she went to make the coffee. Ross was sitting on the sofa when she came back with the tray. He had taken off his jacket and was slumped against the cushions, looking more relaxed than she'd seen him look for ages, and her spirits lifted a little. To know that he felt so at ease in her home was some consolation.

'That was quick. Here, let me take that for you.' He stood up and took the tray from her, setting it down on the stool she used in lieu of a coffee-table. Crouching down beside it, he picked up the pot. 'Shall I pour?'

'If you like.' Gemma sank down on the chair, tucking her feet beneath her as she watched him pour the coffee into two mismatched china mugs she'd found at a rummage sale. He looked up, one dark brow quirking in a way that she found irresistibly attractive.

'Milk? Sugar? I'm ashamed to admit that I don't know how you take your coffee.'

'Not usually your job to do the coffee run,' she teased him and he grinned.

'No. Maybe I should take a turn at it?'

'Best not,' she advised him. 'You don't want the staff worrying that you're having some sort of breakdown if you suddenly take on the role of drinks monitor.'

'Not if it means another round of sympathy,' he said drily. He grinned as he held the milk jug aloft. 'That being the case, this is a one-off-never-to-be-repeated offer, so make the most of it. What's it to be?'

'Just milk, please.'

Gemma accepted the cup, waiting while he added both milk and sugar to his own cup. He resumed his seat, sighing with pleasure as he tasted the coffee.

'This is very good. Where do you buy your coffee?'

'It's just the supermarket's own brand—nothing fancy.'

'Really?' He shook his head. 'I pay extravagant money for mine and it doesn't taste half as good as this. I need to rethink my shopping habits.' Ross drank some more coffee then looked around the room. 'Have you lived here ever since you moved to Dalverston?'

'Almost. I rented a room until I found this place. I didn't think I'd be able to afford it at first, but my parents helped me with the deposit.' She glanced around and smiled. 'That's why I had to be economical with the furnishings. More or less everything in the house has been bought at jumble sales or from charity shops.'

'Well, it doesn't matter where it came from because it looks great,' he said sincerely, and she laughed.

'Thank you. I have to confess that I was a bit nervous about what you would think.'

'Nervous? Why on earth should you feel nervous?'

'Well, I've been to your house and everything is so perfect—there's not a thing out of place.' She gave a little shrug. 'I expected you to turn up your nose at all my clutter.'

'Which is my problem and not yours.' Ross looked sombre as he set his cup on the tray.

'There's nothing wrong with wanting things to be in their rightful places,' she said gently, not wanting him to feel uncomfortable.

'Perhaps not. However, expecting people to respond in a certain way probably isn't the best way to conduct a relationship.'

'You think you put pressure on Heather to conform to your standards?' Gemma suggested, tentatively. Although Ross seemed happy enough to talk, she didn't want to go beyond the boundaries he was comfortable with.

'The truthful answer is I don't know. I just assumed that

Heather wanted what I did, but obviously I was wrong.' His tone was flat and she couldn't help wondering if it was because he was afraid of revealing too much. Ross was a very private person and she was merely a colleague who had been recently elevated to the status of a friend.

It was a timely reminder of how tenuous her position was. Gemma realised that she needed to be extremely careful and not make the mistake of getting too involved in his affairs. Ross might be glad of her support at the moment but everything could change once he had recovered from this setback.

'Maybe you weren't wrong,' she said, hoping he couldn't hear the ache in her voice, an echo of the one in her heart. 'It could be that Heather just got a bad case of cold feet. A lot of brides do.'

'But they don't all call off their weddings, do they?' His smile was wry. 'No, Heather wasn't convinced that she wanted to spend her life with me and I don't blame her. I do tend to take life far too seriously.'

'Then you have to learn to relax,' she said lightly, hating to hear the regret in his voice. It was obvious that Ross blamed himself for the split and that must make the situation even more painful for him. She deliberately adopted an upbeat tone. 'What do you enjoy doing? When you're not working, I mean.'

'Nothing particularly exciting,' he replied with a shrug.

'Oh, come on, there must be something that floats your boat, even if it's a secret addiction to old Laurel and Hardy films. You can tell me. I swear I won't reveal your secrets to anyone, no matter how bizarre they are!'

He laughed out loud. 'I'm not sure it would be wise to

tell you. It could be something to blackmail me with if I confess to some kind of dark and guilty passion.'

'Would I do such a thing?' She tried to look as though butter wouldn't melt in her mouth and probably failed.

Ross shook his head. 'I hate to disappoint you but I honestly and truly don't have any secret likes—or dislikes, for that matter.'

'Fair enough, but if I find out that you're a closet heavy metal fan, I shall rib you unmercifully.'

'I'd better hide my music collection.' Ross returned her smile. 'So what about you? What addictions do you have?'

'Oh, loads! I'm addicted to jumble sales and charity shops. I can't pass a shoe shop without going in and trying on the shoes even if I haven't any intention of buying them. I'm totally addicted to chocolate and could eat a whole box all to myself if I didn't make myself stop. And then there's the singing. That really is an addiction.'

'Singing? You're in a choir?' Ross exclaimed, and Gemma laughed.

'No choir would have me. I have awful difficulty hitting the right note but that doesn't deter me. I sing all the time when I'm at home—when I'm cooking or I'm dusting or vacuuming. But my favourite place is the bathroom. The acoustics in there are wonderful!'

'I had no idea. We've worked together for three years and I never suspected you had this guilty secret in your life.' Ross's eyes danced with laughter. 'You do realise that now I can blackmail you?'

'Ah, but we're friends. And friends don't betray a secret. They guard it with their lives.'

'As I shall guard yours,' he said quietly.

There was a moment when their eyes met, a tiny fraction of time when the world seemed to stop spinning. Gemma felt her heart catch as she looked into Ross's eyes and saw the warmth they held, a warmth that was there for her and for her alone. Then Ross reached for his cup, and everything returned to normal.

They finished their coffee, chatting while they drank. Ross was excellent company and the time flew past. It was only when the old clock on the mantel struck midday that he broke off, looking surprised and a little embarrassed as he checked his watch.

'I didn't realise it was so late. Sorry. I didn't mean to take up so much of your morning, Gemma.'

'There's no need to apologise.' Gemma stood up and placed her cup on the tray. 'I invited you here and I didn't set a time limit on how long you should stay. I've enjoyed this morning.'

'So have I, and not just because it got me away from my mother and her well-meaning attempts to console me.' He gave her a wry smile as he stood up. 'Mum finds it very difficult to believe that her baby boy is all grown up at times.'

'I imagine most mothers are the same. I know mine is,' Gemma said with a laugh, handing him his jacket.

He shrugged it on, drawing her attention to the solid breadth of his chest and the width of his shoulders. Even on a Saturday he was immaculately dressed in a pair of well-pressed cords and a cashmere sweater. Gemma suddenly found herself wondering what he would look like in a pair of jeans, well-worn jeans that would mould his muscular legs, jeans that he would remove when he took her to his bed...

She drove the image from her head. No man was ever going to take her to his bed again, and certainly not Ross. She couldn't bear to see the disgust on his face when he saw her scars, her imperfections. Anger rose up inside her all of a sudden. It wasn't fair that her life should have been ruined through no fault of her own!

Ross zipped up his jacket. He couldn't believe how quickly the time had passed. It seemed only a few minutes since he'd arrived yet he'd been here a couple of hours. Gemma was such easy company and he had enjoyed being with her so much. He would like to spend a lot more time with her, if he was honest.

He swallowed his sigh as he turned to say his goodbyes. At the moment, he needed to get himself back on track and he definitely shouldn't be thinking about starting another relationship. It wasn't fair to Gemma to confuse the issue when she had offered him the hand of friendship. Just because he'd discovered that he was attracted to her, it didn't mean that she reciprocated his feelings. Far from it. Bearing in mind that she was Heather's friend, she would probably be appalled by the idea.

It was a salutary thought. Ross knew that it was time he left before he did something he would regret. He opened his mouth to thank her for her hospitality then stopped when he saw how upset she looked.

'Gemma, what is it?' he said in concern. 'Don't you feel well?'

He laid his hand on her forehead but her skin was cool to the touch, with no sign of fever. It was also satiny smooth and so fine that he let his hand remain there. Gemma didn't say a word as she stared at him with eyes filled with a mixture of pain and anger, and he felt more concerned than ever. Gemma never got angry, so what was wrong with her? Was it something he'd done that had upset her?

He searched his mind but for the life of him he couldn't think of anything that could have caused such a reaction. Bending, he stared into her eyes and saw the exact moment when she focussed on him. He heard her draw a ragged breath and knew that she was struggling to regain control.

'It's all right,' he murmured as he drew her into his arms. 'I don't know what's wrong, but everything will be fine. I promise you that.'

He let his hand slide down her cheek, feeling her skin glide like silk beneath his palm. Although her forehead had been cool to the touch, her cheek felt warm, the faint glaze of colour hinting that she was embarrassed by what had happened, and that was the last thing he wanted.

He pulled her closer, wanting to reassure and comfort her any way he could. She felt so small as she nestled against him and he'd have been a liar if he'd claimed that the feel of her in his arms didn't affect him, but he clamped down on the rush of desire. The very least he could do was offer her a shoulder to cry on after what she had done for him. It was what friends did, wasn't it? They were there for one another and he intended to be there for her too.

They must have stayed like that for well over five minutes, Ross cradling her in his arms, Gemma nestling against him. And then she took a shuddery little breath and stepped back.

'I'm sorry.' She looked up and smiled bleakly. 'You must think I'm crazy. I don't know what came over me…'

She tailed off and he knew it was because she didn't want to lie to him. She *did* know what had upset her but she didn't want to tell him.

'There's nothing to apologise for,' he said quietly, taking hold of her hands because he wanted her to know that he was there if she ever needed to talk. If Gemma chose to share this secret with him, he would do everything in his power to make things right for her.

The force of his feelings shocked him and he gripped her hands. 'If there's anything I can do to help, Gemma, just tell me.'

'Thank you.' Her eyes swam with tears but she smiled as she withdrew her hands. 'I appreciate your kindness, Ross, but I'm fine. Honestly.'

Ross knew that she was a long way from being fine but there was nothing he could do. He certainly didn't intend to upset her even more by forcing her to tell him the truth. He stepped back, needing to set some distance between them, both physically and emotionally. He had to remember that he was trying to get his own life back on track and not confuse matters by getting caught up in Gemma's problems.

'Good. Right, I think I'd better get off now. Thanks again for the coffee and the chat. I enjoyed this morning enormously.'

He bade her a swift goodbye, not lingering on the step when she showed him out. A quick wave as he got into his car and that was that. He drove straight home and went into his study, taking a stack of medical journals off the shelf. He'd been so busy with wedding preparations recently that he'd let things lapse, and he needed to catch up.

He opened the journal at an article about type 1 diabetes, but after a couple of sentences he found his mind drifting. It was Saturday afternoon and surely he could think of something more interesting to do? He ran through a list of options, but nothing appealed. Visiting the cinema on his own was definitely out—think of the sympathetic looks he'd attract if anyone saw him. Ditto the swimming pool which would be full of families anyway.

He could go Christmas shopping, but he couldn't face the thought of the crowds. Anyway, apart from a present for his mother and the usual chocolates for the staff at the surgery, there weren't that many to buy. Last year he'd bought Heather a necklace, but she'd chosen it herself to save him the trouble of looking and he'd merely phoned the shop and paid for it. Maybe the alarm bells should have started ringing then? After all, choosing a present for the woman you loved should be a pleasure rather than a chore.

Ross sighed as he tipped back his chair. It was galling to admit that he had made such a mess of things. His relationship with Heather would never have worked and he was lucky that she had realised it in time. The problem was that he'd been too focussed on his aims as a doctor when he should have paid more attention to how he felt as a man. If he could redress the balance then everything would be fine.

Closing his eyes, he started to create a new picture of his future, complete with a cast of wife, kids and pets. The kids and pets were easy—he could conjure them up in droves. However, picturing the woman who one day would share his dream was a lot harder. A face suddenly began to take shape in his mind's eye—satiny skin, a lush mouth, grey eyes, perfect ears…

His eyes flew open and he picked up the discarded journal. Gemma was his friend. She certainly wasn't the latest candidate for his ideal life partner!

CHAPTER EIGHT

MONDAY morning was always a busy time in the surgery, and at this time of the year, when there were so many coughs and colds about, it was hectic. Gemma had appointments scheduled for every ten minutes and was hard pressed to keep up. When Sarah Roberts arrived for the first of the immunisation shots she needed for a forthcoming holiday in Mexico, Gemma was snatching a quick cup of tea.

'Sorry. It's been madly busy this morning. I was just trying to grab a cuppa before you arrived.'

'Take your time. I'm in no rush,' Sarah told her as she sat down by the desk. She placed her bag on her knee, nervously twisting the strap around her fingers while Gemma finished her tea.

'That's better. I think I might survive now.' Gemma set the mug aside then frowned when she saw how flushed Sarah looked. Although a lot of people were nervous about having injections, it shouldn't have caused this sort of a reaction. 'Are you feeling all right, Sarah? You look rather hot to me.'

'I am a bit.'

Sarah plucked at the scarf tucked into the neck of her

jacket and Gemma was even more concerned when she saw that Sarah's hands were shaking. Reaching across the desk, she checked Sarah's pulse and discovered that it was extremely rapid and very irregular, as was her breathing.

'How do you feel apart from being hot?' she said quietly. If Sarah was sickening for something, it certainly wouldn't be wise to begin her immunisation programme that day.

'Sort of nervy and twitchy, you know.' Sarah laughed and there was a hint of hysteria in her voice. 'I feel all churned up like you do when you've had a shock.'

'And when did this start?' Gemma brought up Sarah's file on the computer. Apart from her weight-loss problem, she had been extremely healthy since she'd joined the practice the previous year.

'This morning, although I felt on edge all weekend, if I'm honest. I know Martin was fed up with me jumping up and down all the time while he was trying to watch the rugby on television,' she added and suddenly burst into tears.

Gemma got up and put her arm around her. 'I think you need to see one of the doctors, Sarah. I'll check who's free. I really don't feel happy about starting your injections today if you're sickening for something. It wouldn't be very sensible, would it?'

'I don't suppose so.' Sarah sighed as she mopped her eyes with a tissue. 'Although Martin will be furious if I don't have my shot today. He's been planning this holiday for ages. I don't want to go, really, because I can't bear the thought of having to strip off if we go to the beach, but Martin refuses to listen to me. He keeps telling me that I should buck up my ideas and stop moaning.' She gave a noisy sniff. 'I don't know why he stays with me. I mean, look at me! I'm so gross that it's no wonder he doesn't fancy me any more.'

Gemma didn't say anything as she reached for the phone. If Sarah's husband tried being a little more sympathetic there might not be a problem, she thought privately. She checked with Carol and discovered that Ross had a cancelled appointment in fifteen minutes' time so booked Sarah in. Once everything was arranged she took the other woman through to the meeting room and let her wait in there rather than return to the reception area while she was upset.

She promised Sarah that she would take her through to see Ross when it was time and went back to her room, trying to curb the feeling of excitement that was making her feel twitchy now too. She'd not seen Ross yet that day but the memory of what had happened on Saturday still loomed large. Ross had seemed so relaxed when he'd been at her house, and she'd found herself responding to him even more than usual. It was only the thought of how horrified he would be if he saw her scars that had brought her down to earth. And what a bumpy landing it had been.

It had been years since she'd felt so angry. Not even when she'd split up with Mike had she felt so overwhelmed by the unfairness of it all. However, on Saturday the pain had been too much to bear. What had made it worse was that Ross had witnessed her distress.

Should she have told him the truth? she wondered, not for the first time. But how could she have told him when it would have meant her explaining everything else—how she'd been thinking about him in those jeans and taking her to his bed…

Heat washed through her and she knew that she couldn't

have risked telling Ross about her accident on Saturday, neither could she tell him in the future either. Although she knew how sympathetic he would be, that wasn't the point. It must remain her secret, one she could never share with him in case it meant she had to share all the others.

Ross had been looking forward to a break after Carol had informed him that his eleven o'clock appointment had cancelled. His list had seemed to be longer than ever that day and those precious few minutes would have been nice. Normally, he worked through his appointments and didn't even think about it, but he felt very on edge that day. He'd felt this way ever since Saturday, too, felt uneasy, distracted, unable to concentrate on the simplest tasks, and it was all down to Gemma and the effect she seemed to be having on him recently. Why was he so acutely aware of her all of a sudden when he had never really noticed her before?

It was impossible to answer that question. When Carol phoned to tell him that she had slotted in another patient, he was relieved. Perhaps he didn't need a breather after all—he needed to concentrate on his job and stop thinking all these crazy thoughts. He ushered out his patient and went back to his desk, not bothering to glance up when there was a knock on the door.

'Come in,' he called, his gaze locked to the computer as he finished updating the previous patient's file.

'Good morning, Dr Mackenzie,' someone said quietly and Ross's head jerked up when he immediately recognised Gemma's voice.

'Good morning, Gemma,' he replied, feeling a smile twitching at the corners of his mouth as he looked at her.

She was dressed in her usual uniform which comprised a navy-blue cotton dress and flat shoes. However, the funny thing was that even though he must have seen her in the outfit hundreds of times before, he'd never realised before how much it suited her. He felt a sudden stirring in his lower body and hurriedly looked away. There was no point fantasising about how the body beneath that crisply laundered cotton would look because he was never going to find out!

He cleared his throat, determined to get a grip on himself and his wayward emotions. 'Did you want to speak to me about a patient?'

'Yes, Sarah Roberts. Carol has slotted her into your list—has she told you?' She carried on when he nodded. 'Sarah was supposed to have the first of her travel immunisation shots this morning. She and her husband are going to Mexico after Christmas so it's the usual—typhoid and hepatitis A. If I'm not mistaken, you signed the authorisation note.'

'I did. Why? Is there a problem about Sarah having the shots?'

'I'm not sure. That's why I thought she should see you before I gave them to her.'

'You'd better sit down and tell me what's worrying you,' Ross said immediately. He waited while Gemma took her seat, clamping down on the spasm of appreciation that reared its naughty little head again as he watched her cross her shapely legs. No fantasising, no imagining, and definitely no lusting!

'It's hard to pinpoint what's wrong, but Sarah doesn't seem like herself today. She's very flushed and her pulse and breathing are both very erratic.'

Gemma frowned as she tried to work out how best to explain and Ross did a bit more heavy-duty clamping when he saw her delicate brows knit together so beguilingly. He had never thought that eyebrows could be erotic, but they could be on the right person, it appeared.

'That's it, is it?' he said quickly because he hated feeling that he wasn't in control. He'd never experienced this problem before and he couldn't understand what was wrong with him now…unless the shock of the previous week's events had knocked his system out of kilter.

It seemed like the most logical explanation and he clung to it, like a drowning man to a life raft. 'She's flushed and has an erratic pulse and breathing? Nothing else?'

'No, except that Sarah mentioned she'd felt very jittery over the weekend, as though she'd had a shock, but it was all very vague, I'm afraid.' Gemma sighed. 'I'm sorry to be so unhelpful but that's all I could get out of her. It's obvious that she's extremely unhappy, though.'

'About her weight?' Ross suggested.

'That's the main reason, although the fact that her husband is less than sympathetic isn't helping. Sarah seems to believe that he no longer finds her attractive because she's overweight.'

'That's a difficult one to resolve.' Ross shrugged when Gemma looked at him questioningly. 'The more upset Sarah is about the state of her marriage, the more she comforts herself by eating, and the problem spirals.'

'If only her husband would reassure her that her weight doesn't matter, it would help.'

'If it's true, yes, it would help. But maybe her weight does matter to him. Maybe he finds it a turn-off.'

'So it's all down to appearance,' she said bitterly. 'Men can only love a woman if she conforms to their idea of perfection.'

Ross frowned when he heard the bitter note in her voice. He had a feeling the comment was based on personal experience, but that didn't make any sense. His gaze skimmed over Gemma and he didn't even attempt to curb the surge his body gave this time. Gemma was gorgeous from the top of her silky head to the tips of her toes in those sensible shoes so what experience could she have of being rejected? He was on the verge of asking her when she stood up.

'I'll fetch Sarah in,' she said coolly as she went to the door.

Ross sat back in his seat, trying to clear his mind so he could concentrate on their patient's problem rather than Gemma's… He sighed. What problem? He was merely speculating that there was a problem and he couldn't possibly be right. His gaze lingered on Gemma as she ushered Sarah into the room. There wasn't a man born who wouldn't want to be with Gemma and keep her by his side, day in and day out. She was perfect in every way and he was only sorry that it had taken him so long to realise that himself.

Gemma got Sarah settled in the chair. She knew there was no reason why she should stay, but she'd seen the pleading look Sarah had given her and didn't have the heart to leave her. Sitting down beside her, she shot Ross an anxious look, but he seemed well aware of the other woman's fragile state of mind.

'Gemma has told me that you've not felt very well over the weekend, Sarah,' he said gently. 'We need to get to the bottom of what may be wrong with you, don't we?'

'Yes.' Sarah bit her lip and Gemma could tell that she was close to tears again.

'There's no need to worry about getting upset, Sarah. Sometimes having a good cry is the best medicine of all.' Ross smiled sympathetically at her. 'Bottling things up causes a lot more damage, believe me.'

'I thought I was going mad,' Sarah admitted, obviously relieved to be able to talk about what was worrying her. 'I feel so jittery, as though every nerve in my body is jangling.'

'Have you taken anything that could have caused this reaction?' Ross looked calmly into Sarah's eyes. 'Some drugs are known to have this kind of an effect and I'd like to rule them out or get you the help you may need.'

'Drugs,' Sarah echoed, then flushed. 'Oh, no, no! I've not taken anything like *that*. I mean, I wouldn't!'

'Good. I'm pleased to hear it, but I had to ask.'

Ross's tone was soothing and Gemma saw Sarah relax again. He was always so good with the patients, she thought, so kind and sympathetic that they couldn't help responding to him. The thought sent a feeling of warmth flooding through her. She couldn't help responding to him either, although it wasn't his sympathy she wanted.

'The first principle of diagnosis is to rule out the obvious and that's what we've just done,' he continued in the same easy tone, and Gemma forced her mind to behave itself. 'I'm going to examine you now, take your blood pressure and ask you a few more questions if that's all right?'

'Yes. Thank you.'

Ross got up and came around the desk. Gemma jumped up and went to fetch the sphygmomanometer off the shelf in the corner. He nodded when she brought it over to him.

'Thanks. Would you do the honours?'

'Of course.'

Gemma wrapped the inflatable cuff around Sarah's upper arm and pumped it up. She took the reading and then repeated it to make sure it was correct. Ross leant over to check the reading and frowned.

'That reading is way too high, although it wasn't a problem on Friday.'

'Sarah's BP has always been very steady,' Gemma agreed, trying not to notice how good he smelled as the spicy scent of shower gel assailed her nostrils.

'Which means this is a very recent occurrence.'

He checked Sarah's pulse next, then listened to her chest, back and front through his stethoscope. Gemma didn't want to disturb him so once she had unfastened the cuff, she stayed where she was, crammed between him and the desk. She tried not to breathe too deeply, not wanting to test her willpower again by drinking in any more of that delicious aroma, only it wasn't just her nostrils that were tingling now. Ross's nearness was having its usual effect on her, but whereas in the past she had been able to control it, it was more difficult now that the mental barriers had been breached. He was no longer Heather's fiancé and it was hard to slot him back into the safe category when she wanted to slot him into a very different one.

'Tell me what you did at the weekend, Sarah.'

Ross finished his examination and resumed his seat. Gemma's legs felt weak as she returned the sphygmomanometer to its rightful place. Being in such close proximity to him had been a test of her self-control but she'd survived.

She went back and sat beside Sarah, determined to focus on this problem.

'Nothing much. I did some housework and shopping, cooked our meals. That's about it.'

'And your husband ate the same food as you did?' Ross persisted.

'Well, no. I have that diet sheet, and Martin isn't keen on salads and things like that,' Sarah replied, sounding flustered. She started plucking at the strap on her bag again and Gemma could tell that she was becoming increasingly agitated.

Ross noticed it as well because he leant forward and looked her in the eyes. 'Is there something you aren't telling us, Sarah? We only want to help you so please don't think that we're going to judge you. Our sole concern is your welfare, isn't that right, Gemma?'

'Yes,' Gemma agreed, turning to the other woman. 'Dr Mackenzie and I want to help you, Sarah.'

Sarah's face suddenly crumpled. 'I think it might be the coffee,' she whispered.

'Coffee?' Gemma repeated, glancing at Ross, who shrugged.

'Yes. I found this diet on the Internet, you see. It said that if you drank lots of very strong coffee it would help you lose weight. Dozens of people had written to the site to say how much weight they'd lost so I thought I'd try it.' She tailed off, tears streaming down her face.

Ross sighed. 'Do you know how many cups of coffee you've drunk?'

'Not really. Several dozen, I suppose. I had five this morning before I came here.'

'And I expect it was strong coffee too, like espresso?' Ross said gently.

'Yes,' Sarah mumbled miserably.

'Then it's pretty clear what's happened. You've overdosed on caffeine. That's why you feel so hot and nervous, and why your heart is racing and your blood pressure is elevated.'

'Overdosed? But it was just coffee!' Sarah exclaimed. 'You make it sound like I've taken some sort of drug!'

'Because that's what caffeine is—a stimulant drug that occurs naturally in coffee beans, tea leaves, cocoa beans and cola nuts. It's classified as a drug to the extent that it's use is banned by athletes taking part in any kind of sporting event.'

'But I had no idea… I mean, everyone drinks coffee,' Sarah protested.

'But not in the quantity that you've been drinking it. A couple of cups of coffee a day—regular strength, mind— is fine. However, more than that can lead to caffeine addiction and there's all the usual side-effects when you stop drinking it—headaches, tremors, sleeplessness, etcetera.'

'I feel so stupid. I had no idea it could do all those things. I just wanted to lose weight as fast as I could.'

'Believe me, Sarah, this isn't the way,' Ross said firmly. 'All you'll do is ruin your health and it's not worth that, is it?'

'No,' Sarah said slowly. 'I don't want to make myself ill. I just want to feel pretty again and know that Martin finds me attractive.'

'Then stick to the diet we've given you,' Ross told her. 'It won't happen overnight because it isn't a miracle cure. But any weight loss will be achieved sensibly and without you endangering your health.'

Sarah nodded. 'You're right. I can't believe how silly I've been. I felt so ill this morning, too. I thought I was dying.'

'You'll feel a lot better once the caffeine works its way out of your system,' Ross assured her. 'Drink plenty of water and get some rest, and you should feel a lot better tomorrow.' He glanced at Gemma. 'I don't think it's wise to start the immunisation programme today so maybe you can reschedule Sarah's appointment for next week.'

'Of course.' Gemma stood up and followed Sarah to the door.

She glanced back when Ross said quietly behind her, 'Well done for recognising there was a problem. Hopefully, we've managed to stop it developing into anything more serious.'

'You mean, *you've* stopped it developing into something more serious,' Gemma countered. Her gaze rested on his handsome face and it felt as though her heart was swelling to double its normal size. He was such a good doctor and such a good person. He deserved to be happy and she would do everything she could to help him win back the woman he loved.

'The credit is all yours, Ross,' she said, forcing down the lump in her throat because she couldn't help wishing that she was that woman. 'I just wish that Heather had seen you with Sarah just now. She would realise exactly what she has lost.'

There wasn't time to say anything else as Sarah was waiting for her. She closed the door and accompanied Sarah to the desk where they set up another appointment for the following week. After that, Gemma had to catch up with her own appointments. She overran, of course, and ended up working through her lunch-break, but it didn't matter. It was better to stay busy, to keep her thoughts centred and not let them wander. She knew where they would have ended up—where they always did, with Ross.

CHAPTER NINE

ANOTHER week passed, the second since his aborted wedding day, and Ross was rostered to work on the Saturday morning. Although a lot of practices closed on Saturdays, Dalverston Surgery opened for emergency appointments only. With there being only two weeks left before Christmas, he didn't expect it to be busy that day, but one couldn't always foretell these things. He arrived for work at his usual time, nodding to Dianne Southern, their new receptionist, as he went in.

'Oh, before you go, Dr Mackenzie, there's been a call.' Dianne handed him a slip of paper. 'Mrs Naylor from Naylor's Farm phoned. She said that her husband wasn't well and could someone pop out to see him.'

'Did Mrs Naylor say what was wrong with him?' Ross asked, wondering how urgent the situation was.

'No.' Dianne frowned. 'Her exact words were that her hubby wasn't feeling too good and she thought he should see the doctor, if it wasn't too much trouble.'

'Right. Can you phone Mrs Naylor back and tell her that I'll call after surgery finishes? And if you could find out a bit more information for me, Dianne, it would help.'

He smiled at the receptionist so she wouldn't think she was being reprimanded. Dianne wasn't to blame. It had been so busy recently that staff training time had been pared to the bone. Picking up a scrap of paper, he jotted down a couple of questions he needed answering and handed it to her. 'This should help. OK?'

'Yes. Thank you, Dr Mackenzie.' She sighed. 'I should have thought to ask her what was wrong with her husband. I feel so stupid now.'

'You're doing fine, Dianne. It's early days and you can't be expected to know everything.'

Dianne seemed reassured by the comment. She was already reaching for the phone as Ross headed to his room. He booted up the computer then looked round when someone tapped on the door and felt his heart lurch when he saw Gemma standing in the doorway.

Since the morning when she had accompanied Sarah Roberts to his room, he had done his best to get himself in hand. He'd succeeded too because there'd been no more fantasising, no lusting, nothing at all untoward. He'd told himself it had been a temporary blip, but he couldn't pretend that his heart wasn't kicking up a storm all of a sudden and it worried him. Why was he reacting this way after being virtually oblivious to Gemma's charms for the past three years?

'Dianne's just spoken to Edith Naylor,' she explained, obviously assuming that she had his attention, which she did, although probably not the kind of attention she expected, and that merely proved his point. He'd had no problem separating his personal and his private life in the past. Even when Heather had called into the surgery to see him, he'd been able to function perfectly well. However, it was much harder with Gemma. Not only was she a colleague but someone he fancied like mad!

The thought turned his tongue to a lump of lead. Fortunately, Gemma didn't seem aware of his dilemma as she continued in the same even tone that could have placed her happily on either side of the fence. She would speak to him like that as merely a colleague, and she would do exactly the same if she fancied him too. Now, that *was* an idea to conjure with!

'Edith told her that Jim had pains in his chest during the night. He claimed it was indigestion, but Edith decided to ring us anyway. Jim did complain of chest pains in the summer, but the treadmill test we persuaded him to take didn't show up anything unusual.'

'I remember,' Ross said, forcing the thought from his mind as he brought up Jim's file on the computer. He skimmed through the results of the treadmill test and nodded. 'You're right. His symptoms pointed towards it being angina, but there was nothing in the test results to indicate that Jim was suffering from it.'

He glanced up, willing himself not to betray how on edge he felt. Gemma didn't find him attractive and he had to get that idea right out of his head. 'These things aren't infallible, though. Angina can come on rapidly or it can develop over a period of time due to other factors like anaemia, for instance.'

He checked the screen again, relieved to see that Gemma's expression reflected only concern for their patient. 'I can't see anything in Jim's file about a blood test being done. Who saw him when he came into the surgery? It isn't clear from this who signed his notes.'

'That locum we had for a few weeks, the one Matt got rid of.' Gemma grimaced. 'He kept bragging about how quickly he got through his list every day, but it was only because he cut so many corners.'

'Well, it appears he cut several corners here,' Ross said bluntly. 'No blood tests were ordered, no thyroid test—thyrotoxicosis is another possible cause of angina pectoris because the excessive production of thyroid hormones makes the heart work harder and faster—not even a cholesterol test. And they're just the basics.'

'Heaven only knows how many other people slipped through the net after he saw them,' Gemma said worriedly.

'It's something that needs checking into.' Ross sighed. 'Apart from the fact that lives may have been put at risk by such slipshod work, the surgery could be sued for negligence if anything happens to one of the patients he saw.'

'Seriously?' Gemma exclaimed.

'Oh, yes. We were responsible for hiring him so we were responsible for the quality of his work while he was here.'

'Matt will have a fit when he finds out.' She groaned. 'He doesn't need this on top of everything else.'

'He certainly doesn't,' Ross said grimly because he couldn't help feeling more than partly to blame for the distress the head of the practice was suffering. Maybe Heather had been the one to cancel the wedding, but he knew in his heart that he'd forced her into taking the decision. The thought galvanised him into action.

'I'm not going to tell Matt just yet. I'll wait until I've gone through the files and have a clearer idea of the situation. There's no point worrying him unnecessarily,' he added when Gemma frowned.

'I suppose not, but it's a massive task. That locum was here for almost two months. He saw an awful lot of patients in that time.'

'I realise that, but it has to be done. Carol saves the daily appointment lists on CD, so I'll use them to check back.' He glanced at the screen again. 'The sooner the better from the look of this file. In fact, I'll make a start on it today, after I've been out to see Jim Naylor.'

'Do you want a hand?' Gemma offered immediately. She shrugged when he looked at her in surprise. There was a hint of colour in her cheeks that made him wonder if she might be regretting her impulsive offer. 'I don't mind helping.'

'Thanks. I appreciate the offer, but it's not fair to expect you to give up your afternoon.'

'Two heads are better than one,' she said firmly. 'I can pull out the files while you check them to make sure everything's been done properly—that should halve the time it takes.'

Ross couldn't fault her logic. 'Well, if you're sure,' he said, still keen to let her off the hook if she wanted an excuse.

'I am.' She checked her watch. 'I'll make a start now, in fact. There's nobody booked in to see me this morning. I'm only here in case someone turns up, so I may as well make good use of my time. We can't afford to hang around from the look of it, can we?'

'No, indeed.'

Ross watched her hurry away then forced his attention back to the job while he read through Jim Naylor's notes again to make sure he hadn't missed anything. There was no sense compounding the locum's errors with some of his own. And no point making any errors when it came to Gemma either.

The thought brought him up short and Ross sighed. He had to face the facts: he was deeply attracted to Gemma but it would be wrong to act on these feelings. For one thing, he couldn't be sure how genuine they were. Even though he was relieved the wedding had been cancelled, it had still been a shock and he probably wasn't thinking as clearly as he usually did. The one thing he was absolutely certain of, though, was that he would never do anything to hurt Gemma. He cared too much about her to risk that happening.

Gemma made a start on the files as soon as she got back to her room. Using the disks Carol had made, she checked the daily appointment diary for the period in question. Fortunately, the locum's lists were shorter than those of the permanent members of staff, but there were still an awful lot of files to go through. She was only part-way through the first week of appointments when Chelsea Jones was brought in to have a badly cut knee dressed.

The four-year-old had fallen over and cut herself on some broken glass. Gemma got the poor little mite onto the couch then pulled on a pair of gloves. Taking a spare glove out of the box, she blew into it and knotted the wrist, then handed the makeshift balloon to Chelsea. Hopefully, it would distract her while she attended to her knee.

'Thanks.' Rosemary, Chelsea's mother, smiled gratefully at Gemma. 'She wouldn't let me look at it. That's why it's still full of grit.'

'Most kids hate it when their mums try to apply a bit of first aid,' Gemma assured her, filling a bowl with warm water. She wet a cotton-wool ball and gently mopped away the dirt and congealed blood. Chelsea was happily banging the balloon on the edge of the couch, so once the cut was clean, Gemma fetched a magnifying glass and checked it for any splinters of glass.

'That seems to be fine. There's no bits of glass in it and that's the main thing. I'll put a couple of butterfly stitches on it to hold it together and a nice big dressing to keep it clean.'

She bathed the child's knee with antiseptic then applied the thin strips of plaster that would hold the edges of the wound together while it healed. Chelsea whimpered a bit but otherwise she was extremely good. Once Gemma had placed a large dressing over the whole knee, she gave the child a hug.

'You are a star patient! I think you deserve a lollipop for being such a brave little girl.' She opened the cupboard where she kept a jar of lollipops and offered it to Chelsea. 'Which colour do you want, sweetheart?'

'Red.'

'Please,' Rosemary reminded her and Chelsea obediently repeated it.

'Please.'

'Here you are.'

Gemma handed her the lolly then checked Chelsea's file to make sure that she'd had her tetanus booster when she'd started school that autumn. 'That's great,' she said, glancing at Rosemary. 'She's had a tetanus booster so everything's covered. Just keep the dressing dry for a day or so while the cut heals.'

'Will do.' Rosemary lifted her daughter off the couch. 'Thanks, Gemma. I was dreading bringing her in case she screamed the place down, but you certainly know how to keep the kids happy. You'll make a brilliant mum one day.'

Gemma laughed off the remark as she saw them out but it was hard not to let it get to her. She loved children and had dreamed of having a family of her own one day. After what had happened with Mike, though, she'd realised it was unlikely to happen. It needed a mother *and* a father to create a baby, and she couldn't imagine any man wanting her to bear his child. One look at her scars and it would put him off for good, as it had done to Mike.

Ross suddenly appeared, showing out an elderly woman who had been brought in by her daughter, and Gemma's heart contracted in pain. She could guarantee that she was never going to be a wife or a mother.

Despite Ross's expectations, the morning turned out to be extremely busy. By the time his final patient left, he had a stack of folders on his desk. He took them to the office, shaking his head when Dianne offered to file them.

'They're not urgent. They can be done on Monday so you get off home now.'

'Thanks. Oh, here's Mr Naylor's notes.' Dianne handed him a buff-coloured folder. 'Gemma said you'd need them for the home visit.'

'I shall. Thank you, Dianne.'

Ross took the notes back to his room, smiling to himself. It was typical of Gemma to be one step ahead of him. She was an excellent nurse as well as a good friend. Deliberately, he placed that thought at the forefront of his mind. Thinking of Gemma as someone he desired really wasn't on.

He tucked the folder into his case then took his coat off the hook. It was a good thirty minutes' drive to Naylor's Farm so he may as well get straight off and have lunch when he got back. He was heading out to the corridor when Gemma appeared, putting on her own coat.

'I'm off to see Jim Naylor,' he informed her as they both paused.

'Oh, right. I was just popping out for a sandwich. D'you want me to get you one while I'm at it? If we're going to make a start on those files, there's no point going home for lunch, is there?'

'No.' Ross hesitated as an idea occurred to him. Should he ask her to go with him to see Jim Naylor and that way they could stop off at a pub on the way back and have lunch there? It seemed a bit rich that she should give up her free afternoon when all she would get in return was a sandwich. On the other hand, was it wise to spend more time with her when he was determined to keep a check on this attraction he felt?

Ross sighed wryly. He was making it appear as though he couldn't *trust* himself to be with Gemma, and that certainly wasn't true. 'How do you fancy coming with me? That way we can stop off at a pub on the way back and have something to eat.' He hurried on when she didn't reply, keen to reassure her about his motives. 'It's my way of saying thanks for working this afternoon.'

'You don't need to take me out to lunch to thank me, Ross. I don't expect it.'

'I know you don't.' He smiled at her, feeling his heart lift as he looked into her beautiful grey eyes and saw the warmth they held. Maybe Gemma didn't fancy him, but she liked him, he could tell.

His smile widened as a rush of pleasure filled him. He hadn't felt this happy in a very long time, oddly enough. 'The fact is that I'd enjoy your company, so will you say yes, Gemma? Please.'

CHAPTER TEN

JIM NAYLOR looked more than a little put out when they drew up in the farmyard. He greeted them with a scowl as they got out of the car.

'Edith had no business phoning you. I'm perfectly all right, or I would be if folk would stop all this fussing.'

Gemma hid her smile. Jim was typical of a lot of the older men who farmed the land around Dalverston. They viewed seeing the doctor as a sign of weakness. It had taken her a while to understand their attitude when she'd joined the practice, but now she admired their determination even though she may not agree with it.

'It's not fussing, Mr Naylor. If one of your ewes was sick, you'd call in the vet.' Ross looked the other man in the eyes. 'You should be glad your wife thinks as much of you as you do about your sheep.'

'Aye, well, that's as may be,' Jim conceded, grudgingly. He stepped aside. 'You may as well come in seeing as you're here, although I don't know why it needs two of you. More fuss, that's what it is.'

'Oh, I'm just along for the ride,' Gemma assured him as she went into the kitchen. 'Dr Mackenzie offered to buy me lunch on the way back if I came with him. It was too good an offer to miss.'

'Worth having to listen to this old goat moaning on about nothing,' Edith said pithily. She winked at Gemma. 'It's me who should be seeing the doctor after what I have to put up with. No wonder my hearing isn't what it was.'

'We could arrange for you to have a hearing test,' Gemma suggested with a smile as she undid her coat.

'What, and have to hear every single word he says?' Edith shook her head, her lined face filled with laughter. 'The only reason I'm still sane is because I can't hear half his moans and groans so I think I'll pass on the offer. Right, then, how about a cup of tea for you both?'

'That would be lovely. Thank you.'

Gemma sat down as Ross started asking Jim some questions. She'd been surprised when he had suggested they should have lunch together. However, once he had explained his reasoning, she had understood why. It was his way of thanking her and as long as she didn't get carried away by the idea that he enjoyed her company, there wouldn't be a problem.

'How bad were these pains, Jim?' Ross asked, taking his sphygmomanometer out of his case.

'No worse than a bit of indigestion,' Jim said brusquely. 'They certainly weren't bad enough to call you out here.'

He cast a belligerent look at his wife, who ignored him. Gemma knew the elderly couple thrived on their daily spats, and would be lost without each other.

'Let's not go down that route again,' Ross said firmly as he checked Jim's BP. 'Well, your blood pressure is fine so there's no worries on that score. Can you describe the pain for me? Where exactly was it and how long did it last?'

'It was more like a feeling of pressure than pain,' Jim admitted. 'It was right here, in the centre of my chest, and it must have lasted about five minutes.'

'It kept on for twenty-five minutes,' Edith corrected him. She shook her head when Jim opened his mouth. 'Don't bother telling me I'm wrong because I timed it, from the moment you started complaining to when you told me to stop fussing, and it was twenty-five minutes all told.'

'Good. I'm glad we've established that. So apart from the feeling of pressure were there any other symptoms? Nausea, dizziness, sweating, breathlessness, for instance?' Ross continued, ignoring the couple's bickering.

Gemma had always admired the way he could remain so focussed. It was what made him so good at his job, this ability he possessed to keep his mind centred on the task he was performing. She frowned when she saw him suddenly fumble with his pen because he definitely didn't appear as focussed as he usually did that day. What was bothering him? The thought of the problems they might uncover when they checked those files, or something else, something to do with her, perhaps?

Gemma bit her lip as a feeling of excitement swirled inside her. To imagine even for a second that she might feature in Ross's thoughts made her feel incredibly ener-gised. Maybe they could only be friends, but it was good to know that he wasn't indifferent to her.

Ross picked up his pen and put it back in his pocket. He was all fingers and thumbs today, and it was all down to

Gemma. He couldn't believe how aware of her he felt as he continued asking Jim a series of routine questions. Gemma must have sat in on dozens of examinations over the time they'd worked together, but he'd never been so conscious of her presence before.

'How many times have you experienced this before, Jim?'

'I don't have time to write down each time I get a twinge,' Jim grumbled. 'There's too much to do around this place.'

'So I'll take it that it wasn't a one-off,' Ross said equably, refusing to let the old man's stubbornness throw him off course. When it came to recalcitrant patients, he could hold his own—it was only with Gemma that he seemed to have this problem.

The thought triggered another rush of unease. Taking out his pen again, he made a note on Jim's file to the effect that it wasn't the first time the farmer had experienced chest pains since his last visit to the surgery. Glancing up, he happened to catch Gemma's eye and felt heat run along his veins when she looked away. Was Gemma as aware of him as he was of her? he wondered.

'I think the best plan is to do some tests.' He cleared his throat, wishing he could do the same to his mind. He didn't need ideas like that popping into his head all the time. 'They should point us in the right direction.'

'If you think I'm going for another one of them there treadmill tests, you can think again!' Jim glared at him. 'Waste of time, it was. I walk up and down these hills, day in and day out, and nothing ever happens. Those machines are for city folk, them whose idea of exercise is an hour spent at an expensive gym. I spend every day of my life exercising!'

'I'm not proposing you should have another stress test at the moment.' Ross popped Jim's notes into his case. 'Although I'm not ruling it out either.' He held up his hand when Jim went to interrupt. 'Hear me out first. I want to take some bloods for testing—check to see if you're anaemic or have a problem with your thyroid. I can't do it today because the sample will need to be sent to the lab and there's no collection service at the weekend.'

'I can't come into the surgery,' Jim said smartly when Ross drew breath. 'The weather's on the turn and I need to get my ewes down off the hills before the snow comes. I don't want them dropping their lambs out in the open.'

'I understand that.' Ross turned to Gemma, relieved that his reaction to her didn't appear to be anything unusual now. It had been another blip, he told himself firmly, a minor glitch that wouldn't happen again. 'Could you do the honours, Gemma? I know the district nurses' team should do it, but they're really struggling now that two of their team have gone on maternity leave. It will be easier if we handle this ourselves.'

'Of course I don't mind.' Gemma smiled at Jim. 'The courier comes at lunchtime so I'll call in here first thing Monday morning. Around seven all right?'

'Aye, I suppose so, although if you're later than that, I can't promise to be here.'

'He'll be here, love,' Edith put in. 'I'll tie him to that chair if need be, stubborn old goat. He's not got the sense he was born with, if you ask my opinion.'

'Nobody's asking your opinion, are they?' Jim retorted.

Ross shook his head as he stood up. 'We'll leave you to your discussion, then. Thanks for the tea, Edith.'

'Thank you for coming, Dr Mackenzie,' she replied. 'I appreciate your visit even if someone else doesn't.'

Ross sighed as they left the couple bickering and headed out to the car. 'They're real characters, aren't they?'

'They are indeed.' Gemma grinned as she slid into the passenger seat. 'They think the world of one another, though, despite all their squabbling.'

'You really think so?' he said in surprise, and she laughed.

'Of course they do!'

'I'll take your word for it.' He drove out of the farmyard, taking his time as he negotiated the ruts in the track. 'A couple of times I found myself wondering how they'd stayed married for so long if they've spent all their time arguing.'

'It's a sort of shorthand for their real feelings,' she assured him.

'Is it?' He frowned. 'It's odd that you think that when you were so critical of Sarah Roberts's husband who does virtually the same thing.'

'Ah, but that's different. Sarah's husband undermines her confidence. By constantly showing her that he finds her unattractive, he's hurting her.' She smiled at him. 'Jim and Edith would never deliberately hurt one another.'

'You're wasting your talents by working at the surgery.' Ross grinned at her, basking in the warmth she exuded. There was something about Gemma that made him feel very relaxed and at peace with the world. 'You should be an agony aunt. You could earn a fortune writing a column for one of those glossy women's magazines.'

'Ask Aunt Gemma,' she suggested, chuckling, and he laughed.

'Yep. Spot on.'

Ross allowed himself another quick bask in her warmth then returned his attention to finding them somewhere to eat. It was too soon to start thinking that he and Gemma might become more than friends—far too soon. He had just been through a very unsettling period in his life and he couldn't afford to let his emotions run away with him. He'd been so sure that he and Heather had been suited, but he'd been wrong. If he needed proof of how shaky his judgement was, he only needed to remember that.

It was deflating to face such facts but Ross knew it was essential that he did so. He found a pub a few miles further up the road that served lunch and parked the car. It wasn't very busy and they had their choice of tables. They opted to sit in the snug, choosing a table near the fire. Gemma sighed as she stretched out her hands to the blaze.

'Mmm, that's lovely. It's so cold today. I wonder if Jim was right about it snowing?'

'There was nothing on the weather forecast,' Ross said, lifting a couple of menus off the end of the bar. He handed her one then stretched his feet towards the blaze. 'Tell me if you can smell burning shoe leather, will you?'

'I shall,' she promised, laughing.

She opened her menu, but it was several seconds before Ross followed suit. He was too entranced by the way the firelight flickered on her hair to think about something as mundane as food. She'd told him that she didn't have a boyfriend, yet he found it hard to believe that she was single. Although now that he thought about it, he had never heard any mention of her going out with anyone during the whole time she'd worked at the surgery. How odd. To his mind, men should have been queuing up to take her out so he could only assume that it had been Gemma's decision not to date and he couldn't help wondering why. Had something happened in the past that had made Gemma wary of getting involved?

All of a sudden, Ross knew that he needed to find out what had gone on, and that he needed to do so for all sorts of reasons he had no intention of exploring. It would be simpler and less stressful to accept that Gemma interested him and leave it at that.

It was hard to decide what she fancied eating when everything on the menu looked so delicious. Gemma glanced up, wanting to know what Ross was having, and felt her heart lurch when she found him staring at her with the strangest expression on his face.

'I'll have the lamb shank in red wine gravy.' He closed his menu and smiled at her, and she blinked. Had she imagined that expression on his face, or had Ross *really* been looking at her as though she was the most fascinating person he had ever seen?

'I…um… That sounds good to me. Let's make it two, shall we?'

She hurriedly pulled herself together as he got up to order their food. She had to stop all this nonsense before it got completely out of hand. Of course Ross didn't find her fascinating! Why should he? He'd seen her almost every day for the past three years and he must know her, inside out.

Gemma felt a little calmer by the time he came back with two glasses of orange juice. He placed them on the table, grimacing when it tipped to one side, spilling a dollop of the juice into her lap. 'Sorry! I didn't realise the table had a wonky leg. Here, mop yourself up while I sort it out.'

He handed her a paper napkin then crouched down and wedged a folded beer mat under the table leg. Gemma obediently mopped at the stain on her skirt, although her heart really wasn't in it. Ross was kneeling in front of her, his head bent as he wedged the coaster under the table leg. He was so close now that she could reach out and touch him, run her fingers through that crisp black hair…

A tiny murmur escaped her and he looked up, his blue eyes sharpening as they landed on her face. Gemma wasn't sure what he saw there, but she watched a rim of colour edge his cheekbones as he swiftly rose to his feet. He resumed his seat, taking a long swallow of his drink before he spoke, but even then his voice sounded unnaturally husky.

'That should do the trick. The table shouldn't wobble now with a bit of luck.'

'Good. I'd hate to add gravy to this mess,' Gemma said lightly.

Picking up her glass, she let a little of the cool liquid trickle down her throat. Ross was staring into the fire now as though entranced by the sight, although there was something a little too studied about his absorption. He glanced round then quickly looked away again when he caught her eye, and Gemma's heart began to race. Was Ross trying to disguise the fact that he was attracted to her?

CHAPTER ELEVEN

Ross could feel his stomach churning. He knew he'd given himself away and he had no idea what to do. Gemma had given him no reason to think that she was attracted to him…apart from the way she smiled at him with such warmth, and the way she listened so intently to his every word.

He stamped down on the reasons that were suddenly lining up inside his head. He was trying to justify his behaviour by claiming that Gemma reciprocated his interest and it wasn't fair. As far as she was concerned, he was a friend and a colleague, and most definitely not a potential lover! He took another gulp of his drink as heat surged through him. He could feel his skin burning and prayed that his heightened colour would be attributed to their proximity to the fire, but just to make sure, he scooted his chair back a couple of inches.

'It's getting warm in here,' he said, relieved to hear that he sounded almost normal.

'It is.'

Gemma moved her chair further away from the blaze, although he had a feeling that she was merely humouring him. Had she realised what was going on, worked out that he was attracted to her? he wondered. The thought sent his mind into a spin so it was a relief when the waitress arrived at that moment with their lunch because it provided a welcome distraction.

'Hmm, this is delicious. The gravy is gorgeous.' Gemma popped a morsel of lamb into her mouth while Ross tried to get a grip. No way was he going to disgrace himself by panicking.

'It is good,' he agreed, doing his best to behave as though nothing had happened. He popped a chunk of lamb into his mouth, but he was overwhelmingly conscious of the tension in the air and knew that he had to put a stop to it before it was too late.

Too late for what? a small voice whispered in his inner ear. Too late to pretend that he didn't want Gemma? Too late to stop this attraction developing any further? Too late to stop himself wishing that he and Gemma might have a future together?

Ross's heart sank because it was already too late for any of those things. He *did* want Gemma; he *was* attracted to her; he *longed* for them to be together. He could pretend all he liked, but it wouldn't make a scrap of difference. He was falling head over heels in love with her and there was nothing he could do about it, too.

Gemma popped another piece of meat into her mouth. Quite frankly, it could have been a lump of lead for all she cared. The tension in the air was almost tangible; she had the craziest feeling that if she lifted her hand, she would see it slicing through all the emotions that were whirling around. Were they all Ross's doing, or hers? Or were they both to blame? Was Ross feeling the same as she was, keyed up and on edge, as though she was on the verge of something momentous happening?

The piece of meat suddenly caught in her throat and she coughed as she tried to dislodge it, then coughed again when it didn't shift. She was aware of Ross leaping to his feet, but she couldn't speak. Just getting sufficient air into her lungs was difficult enough.

'Sit up straight.'

He sat her bolt upright then thumped her between the shoulder blades with the heel of his hand, and the piece of meat shot out of her gullet. Fortunately, Gemma had a napkin over her mouth and was spared the embarrassment of having it land on the table, but she would have felt better if the incident hadn't happened. She dredged up a smile so that he wouldn't feel he had to continue ministering to her.

'That did the trick. I'm sorry about interrupting your lunch.'

'Are you sure you're OK?'

He ignored her attempts to dismiss him as he crouched beside her chair. His blue eyes were filled with concern as he searched her face and Gemma felt a little ripple run along her veins, the first stirrings of a passion she had never wanted to experience again. Tears sprang to her eyes because it was so unfair that she could never allow herself to feel like a real woman, could never want a man or allow herself to be wanted by him; could never watch the love in his eyes turn to desire as he looked at her in the seconds before they made love…

'Hey, it's all right. There's nothing to get upset about. I know it must have given you a fright, but you're fine now.'

Ross's voice was so tender, so gentle, that more tears gathered and slid down her cheeks. He had no idea why she was crying and she couldn't tell him—that was the worst thing. He gave a soft groan as he gathered her into his arms, rocking her as though she was a child in need of comfort, and the odd thing was, that was how she felt. She needed to be held and told that everything would be fine even if it never could be. For a few precious minutes she wanted to pretend that she was normal, perfect, capable of being desired.

Gemma wrapped her arms around his waist and clung to him as the pain of the past seven years suddenly overwhelmed her. She cried for everything she'd lost as well as everything she could never have—a husband to love her, children they would both love together. And all the time Ross held her, held her to his heart, and made her feel as though it was the only place he wanted her to be.

When he bent and kissed her on the mouth, softly and with great tenderness, she didn't protest. She was past the point of being sensible, didn't care that the kiss could never lead anywhere. She simply kissed him back and revelled in the warmth of his mouth, the feel of his strong body, the sense of security he had wrapped around her like a blanket. For a few precious moments, she had everything she had ever wanted—she felt loved.

Ross could feel his heart drumming. Thump, thump, thump, like a big bass drum. Its beat shook him, made him tremble, and he didn't give a damn. So what if Gemma could feel what this kiss was doing to him? The world wouldn't stop, the ground wouldn't open beneath him, and he wouldn't drop down dead. Ever since he'd been a child, he'd held back, given bits of himself, never too much, but not any more. Definitely not now!

He pulled her closer and groaned when he felt her breasts pushing against his chest. Gemma was all woman, her body softly rounded, deliciously shaped as he cradled her against him. Their bodies seemed to be made for each other, fitting together so perfectly, and this was only for starters. How much better would they fit when he took her to his bed and made love to her?

Heat invaded every cell in his body. He had to draw back so he could suck in enough air to keep his lungs functioning and suddenly he had a perfect view of Gemma's face. Her eyes were closed, her mouth swollen and red from passion as well as his kisses. Gemma looked exactly like a woman should look when she was being made love to and the thought made him want to punch the air for joy. He might not have planned that this would happen, but he didn't regret it. It wasn't a mistake!

'Oops, sorry. I'll come back later.'

The waitress's hasty apology brought Ross back to earth with a thump. He let Gemma go and shot to his feet, realising all of a sudden that the snug of the local pub wasn't the best place for what had been happening. Gemma ran a trembling hand over her hair, her cheeks ablaze with colour at the thought of them being caught if not quite in flagrante delicto then at least on the verge of it, and Ross grimaced.

'A timely intervention, wouldn't you say?'

'Y-es.'

She quickly averted her eyes and he realised that he

couldn't live with himself if she was embarrassed by what had happened. Sitting down at the table, he reached for her hand.

'I'm not going to apologise, Gemma. I wanted to kiss you and I have no intention of pretending it was some sort of accident. OK?'

'Yes.'

She gave him a quick smile then applied herself to her lunch, leaving him feeling as though he was floundering in quicksand. He'd just admitted that he'd wanted to kiss her, but she hadn't reciprocated, so what did it mean? That she was indifferent to what had happened?

Ross found that very difficult to believe bearing in mind the way she had kissed him back. Apparently, she was reluctant to say too much about her feelings and he had no idea why. Gemma was always so open and candid that her sudden restraint puzzled him. Why was she holding back?

He was no closer to solving the problem by the time they finished their lunch. Gemma thanked him politely and got into the car, leaving him feeling more perplexed than ever as he climbed in beside her. He sighed softly. Although he didn't regret kissing her, he would regret it if he had damaged their precious friendship.

By the time they arrived back at the surgery, Gemma had managed to pull herself together. Maybe it had been a shock when Ross had kissed her, but surely it had been just the natural progression carrying on from what had just happened. She'd choked on that piece of meat, Ross had rushed to her aid, and one thing had led to another. The best thing she could do now was to put it out of her mind.

'I've made a list of all the files we need to check,' she

told him as they went into the office. He whistled as she handed him the list.

'It's even longer than I thought it would be. I doubt we'll be able to get through all these files today.'

'We'll have to carry on tomorrow,' Gemma said, trying to stifle her qualms at the thought of spending the entire weekend with him after what had happened. This was work related, and that made a world of difference.

'I can't expect you to give up your weekend to sort out this mess. It isn't fair, Gemma. There must be loads of things you'd rather be doing.'

'Nothing that can't be put off.' She gave a little shrug when she saw the scepticism on his face. 'It's true. There's nothing urgent that needs my attention. I'm happy to help.'

'It's very good of you, but it doesn't seem fair to take such a huge chunk out of your weekend. I know you said that you weren't dating at the moment, but at this time of the year, there must be all sorts of social events in the pipeline. I don't want to mess up your plans.'

'You aren't,' she said shortly, not wanting to explain that she didn't have any plans. Although she went out with friends to the theatre or the cinema occasionally, she spent most of her free time at home. She certainly never dated because there was no point when it could never lead anywhere. Whenever any of her friends asked her why there was no one special in her life, she avoided giving them a direct answer. She'd never even told Heather the truth, but had let her believe that she dated occasionally and left it at that. It was much simpler than explaining her decision to remain celibate.

'Well, if you're sure it won't cause a problem?' Ross

insisted, and she swallowed her groan, wishing he would let the subject drop. At the moment he saw her as a normal woman, a woman he'd been tempted to kiss, but she knew how quickly his view of her would change if he found out about her accident.

'It won't,' she said firmly, hurrying to the door. 'I'll just pop the kettle on. We could do with some coffee while we work.'

She didn't wait for him to reply as she made her way to the kitchen. Ross was studying the monitor when she went back—he didn't look up as she placed a mug of coffee beside him and Gemma breathed a sigh of relief. She hated deceiving him, but telling him the truth was out of the question.

Normally, Ross would have had no difficulty focussing on the task at hand. He knew how important it was that they establish which patients might be at risk, but no matter how hard he tried to dismiss the question hanging over Gemma's love life, it wouldn't go away. He simply couldn't understand why she wasn't seeing anyone. It certainly couldn't be because she had a problem with men. That kiss they had shared had ruled out that possibility!

He took a deep breath to calm his racing pulse and crossed the first patient's name off the list. He keyed in the next patient's details and waited for the file to appear. The patient in question, Alison Bradshaw, had seen the locum after discovering a lump in her left breast. Ross's heart sank as he read the notes the locum had made at the time. He had diagnosed Alison as suffering from fibroadenosis—an excessive growth of glandular and fibrous tissue in the breasts which causes lumps. There was nothing wrong with the diagnosis, and it could very well be correct. However, the locum had failed to send Alison for a mammogram to rule out the possibility of breast cancer.

'We need to get Alison Bradshaw back in as soon as possible.' Ross said, deliberately keeping his expression neutral as he glanced at Gemma. Why had she kissed him like that if she was indifferent to him? It didn't add up. 'She had a lump in her left breast which the locum diagnosed as fibroadenosis, but he didn't send her for a mammogram.'

'I'll phone her first thing Monday morning,' Gemma said, making a note on her pad. She lent forward so she could read Alison's phone number off the screen and Ross sucked in his breath when she accidentally brushed against him.

'Sorry.'

She drew back abruptly and he felt more confused than ever. Was she regretting what had happened at lunchtime, wishing she had put a stop to it sooner?

'I'll phone her myself,' he said curtly because the idea didn't sit well with him. Gemma had kissed him without a qualm earlier in the day, but, apparently, she was having second thoughts now, and he couldn't help feeling hurt. 'Don't forget that you're due at Naylor's Farm first thing on Monday morning. I don't want to give Jim an excuse not to have those blood tests done.'

'Fine. Whatever you want to do.'

She made a note on her pad to that effect. Ross returned to the job at hand, checking another dozen or so files in silence. There was a query with the next patient so they made a note of the name, then found another couple of potential problems that would need investigation straight after that. The list was growing by the hour; by the time six o'clock came around they had over two dozen names on it and every single person would need to be recalled and re-examined.

'It's a complete shambles!' Ross stood up, feeling anger swirling around inside him. It was rare he ever lost his temper but he was close to doing so now. 'We're only halfway through the list and look how many recalls we've found.'

'It is worrying,' Gemma agreed, frowning down at her notepad. Her hair fell forwards across her cheek and she tucked it behind her ear in that way he was starting to know so well.

Why had he never noticed it before? he marvelled. He must have been walking around with his eyes closed, oblivious to what had been happening around him. He certainly wasn't oblivious now. Every time Gemma did it he felt his stomach muscles bunch, his nerves tingle, his...

He swung round before he started drooling like an over-sexed schoolboy! 'We can't keep this to ourselves any longer. I'll have to tell Matt what we've uncovered. This kind of slipshod work could have serious repercussions for the practice.'

'But it isn't our fault that locum wasn't up to the job,' Gemma protested. 'Matt hired him through a reputable agency and they checked his references—they were fine.'

'I'm sure they were, but who's to say he hasn't done shoddy work at other practices and they haven't noticed it yet? It was pure chance that we happened to spot the mistake he'd made by not ordering those blood tests for Jim Naylor.'

'You mean, you spotted it, Ross. I doubt many GPs would have picked up on it so quickly.'

Ross felt his heart lift when she smiled at him. She had

this way of looking at him that made him feel incredibly special. Could she have looked at him that way if she didn't care? Could she have kissed him the way she'd done if she hadn't wanted him?

Everything kept coming back to that. Gemma had kissed him as though she'd really meant it and she wouldn't have done that if she was indifferent to him. He wasn't sure why she was so reluctant to admit it. Maybe she was wary of saying too much because of Heather. She probably thought he was still in love with her best friend and felt guilty about what they had done.

Ross felt a wave of tenderness wash through him. Gemma had no need to worry on that score. He wasn't in love with Heather and the sooner he made that clear to Gemma the better.

CHAPTER TWELVE

IT STARTED to snow at six a.m. on Monday morning. Gemma was eating her breakfast when she saw the first flakes drifting down from the sky. She hurriedly finished her toast and stood up. Experience had taught her how quickly the weather could deteriorate and she didn't want to find herself stuck out at Naylor's Farm.

Ten minutes later she set off. She put her case in the boot, adding a spade and a blanket as well. At least she could attempt to dig herself out if she did get stuck and, if that didn't work, the blanket would stop her freezing to death until help arrived. The last thing the practice needed was her getting into difficulties.

Gemma sighed as she pulled away from the kerb. The list she and Ross had started to compile on Saturday had doubled in size by the time they had finished on Sunday afternoon. Ross had sounded very grim as he had informed her that he was going straight round to Matt's house after they left the surgery. He'd clearly been worried about what they had discovered, although she suspected it hadn't been the only thing bothering him. Was he still brooding about that kiss? she wondered for the umpteenth time. Wishing it hadn't happened because he felt guilty about kissing her when it was Heather he loved? Her heart sank at the thought. The sooner they both forgot about it, the better.

Gemma tried to shake off the thought of how difficult it was going to be to forget it as she left the town. The snow was starting to stick now, making driving extremely hazardous. She came to a junction and slowed down, applying the brakes as gently as possible, but even so she felt the car slew sideways. Fortunately, there was very little traffic about. She only saw one other vehicle, an expensive sports car that came tearing along the road. Gemma shook her head as it roared past her. Obviously, the driver was making no concessions for the weather.

Jim Naylor opened the door as soon as he heard her draw up in the yard. 'You folk must have nothing better to do if you're prepared to drive all the way up here in weather like this,' he said shortly as Gemma got out of the car.

'Oh, I can't think of anything better than seeing you, Jim,' she replied cheerily, following him into the kitchen. Edith was standing by the stove and she chuckled when she heard the comment.

'You're not going to frighten her off, Jim, so you may as well accept that you're going to have to have those blood tests done.' She winked at Gemma. 'He's a bit sensitive when it comes to blood, if you catch my drift, love.'

'Really?' Gemma hid her smile. 'There's really no need to worry, Jim. It will be over in a matter of seconds.'

'Take no notice of what she says.' Jim hooked a thumb in his wife's direction and scowled. 'Talking out the top of her head, she is, and that's a fact. I don't have any problem with giving you some blood.'

'Good. I'm pleased to hear it.' Gemma opened her case and took out a syringe and the vials she would need. She placed them in a dish then smiled at the farmer. 'If you'd sit down and roll up your sleeve for me, please, I'll get it done straight away.'

Jim sat down abruptly on a chair. He looked a little pale as he rolled up his shirtsleeve. Gemma swabbed his skin then fastened the tourniquet around his upper arm. 'You'll just feel a sharp prick,' she explained, sliding the needle into the vein. The blood had just started to flow into the vial when Jim suddenly slumped sideways.

'Happens every time,' Edith assured her, grabbing hold of him. 'He's not so bad when it comes to the sheep—he just about manages then. But if he ever cuts himself… Well!'

Edith shook her head in exasperation, although Gemma could tell she was concerned. She hurriedly filled the vials with enough blood to complete all the tests they needed then removed the needle and pressed a cotton-wool ball against the incision. By that time, Jim was starting to come round, looking both woozy and embarrassed by what had happened.

'I don't know what came over me,' he muttered. 'Must be because I've not had my breakfast yet.'

'I'm always telling you that you need something solid in your stomach before you go out tending them there sheep,' Edith admonished him. She went back to the stove, smiling conspiratorially at Gemma as she cracked a couple of eggs into the frying pan.

'No wonder you felt dizzy if you've not had anything to eat,' Gemma concurred, touched by the way Edith had handled the situation. It was exactly as she'd explained to

Ross—Edith and Jim really cared about one another, and neither would set out to hurt the other.

The thought of Ross made her heart leap and she busied herself with filling in the details on the vials so she wouldn't start churning everything over again. Edith invited her to have breakfast with them but Gemma refused. The snow was getting heavier and she wanted to get back to town as soon as she could.

She left the farm and headed back to the main road. The gritter lorry had been out and that made driving a little easier, although it was slow progress, all the same. She drove for about fifteen miles then rounded a bend and gasped at the sight that met her. The sports car that had passed her earlier that morning was lying on its roof in the ditch. The gritter lorry had also come to grief and had ended up on its side in a field. A mountain of salt and sand had spilled out of the back and was blocking the road, creating a hazard for any vehicles travelling along the road. There was no sign of either driver, although the accident must have happened some time before. It meant there might be two people badly injured.

Gemma took out her mobile phone, groaning when she discovered that she couldn't get a signal. Shoving it into her pocket, she got out of her car and ran to the sports car. The driver was hanging, upside down, from his seat belt, and appeared to be unconscious. Gemma tried to open the door to check on him but the car's automatic locking system prevented her gaining entry.

Leaving the car for a moment, she hurried to the lorry, scrambling over the mound of salt and sand that blocked her way. The driver was slumped across the front seat.

There was a large gash on the side of his head and he was bleeding profusely from it. However, when she opened the door of the cab and examined him, she discovered that his pulse was strong and that he was breathing steadily. Although she couldn't rule out the possibility of a head injury, his vital signs were encouraging.

She ran back to her car and found the blanket then took it back to the lorry and covered the driver with it. There was little else she could do for him so that left her with the problem of how to get into the sports car. In the end, she used the spade to shatter the windscreen, then took off her jacket and wrapped it around her hand while she made a large enough hole so she could reach in and check if the man was alive. He was—just—although his pulse was very rapid and thready, and the seat belt was restricting his breathing. He desperately needed help if he was to survive.

Gemma put her coat back on and looked round. The snow was falling in thick white sheets now, blotting out the surrounding countryside. She was too far away from Naylor's Farm to drive all the way back there and use their phone, so her best plan was to find a signal for her mobile. Hopefully, she would get a better reception if she climbed up one of the hills. She cast a last look at the vehicles and set off, hoping she wouldn't have to climb too far. She didn't rate her chances of finding her way back in this weather if she got lost.

It was barely seven a.m. when Ross drove into the surgery car park. Although his first patient wasn't due until eight, he'd arranged to meet Matt there before everyone arrived so they could go through the suspect files. It would be up to Matt what happened after that, although Ross guessed that the head of the practice would contact every patient and arrange for them to be seen. All he could hope was that nobody would end up paying for the locum's errors.

He let himself in and switched off the alarm. He was just going into the office when Matt appeared, looking grim-faced as he bade Ross a curt good morning. Ross didn't take it personally. He knew the older man was extremely concerned about what had happened, and that it couldn't have come at a worse time, either. Following on from the wedding fiasco, it must be a nightmare for him.

'Let's get straight down to it.' Matt followed him into the office and pulled up a chair. 'We'll need to call back all the patients who have a query about their treatment. I'd like them to be seen within the next couple of weeks, too. What I don't want is for people to be hanging about over Christmas and the New Year.'

'It's going to be a major task to fit them all in,' Ross warned him.

'I realise that, but it has to be done.' Matt smiled grimly. 'I don't need my professional life turning into a shambles as well as my private life.'

Ross didn't say anything. He was very aware that he was more than partly to blame for all the recent disruptions. If only he'd realised the mistake he'd been making by asking Heather to marry him, he thought sadly as he brought up the list of suspect files. His mind flickered to Gemma, to the fact that it wouldn't be a mistake to ask her to marry him, before he brought it back in line. It was too soon for that. He needed to make sure that Gemma knew the truth about his relationship with Heather first, and it might take some time to convince her that he had never been in love with her friend. She was bound to have doubts, to wonder if he was on the rebound, but somehow he had to make her believe him.

It was worrying to know what a difficult task lay ahead. Ross deliberately pushed it to one side and the next hour flew past. He and Matt were still hard at work when Carol arrived.

'My, you two are keen!' she exclaimed. She glanced at the screen and frowned. 'I don't remember setting up that list.'

'You didn't,' Matt explained tersely. 'Ross and Gemma did it over the weekend.'

'Oh, I see,' Carol murmured, looking a little put out. As practice manager, Carol was in charge of the paperwork and normally she would have been involved in something like this from the outset. Ross hurried to explain that it hadn't been a deliberate attempt to undermine her position.

'Something cropped up on Saturday morning that alerted us to the fact that there could be a problem with some of the patients who were seen by that locum we hired in the summer. Gemma and I checked through the files over the weekend and it appears he was cutting corners by not ordering certain tests and procedures to be carried out.'

'Really?' Carol couldn't hide her dismay. 'But that's awful!'

'It is,' he agreed, relieved that he had managed to smooth things over. This was going to cause enough upset in the practice without Carol's feathers being ruffled as well.

He left Matt and Carol discussing what needed to be done and went to his room. His morning list was on his desk and he glanced through it while he kept one eye on the door. Gemma had to pass his door on her way to the nurses' room and he wanted to know how she had got on at Naylor's Farm.

He sighed because that was just an excuse. The truth was that he wanted to see her, talk to her and watch her smile. He had never felt this strongly about anyone before and it was a revelation to feel this sense of longing. Did Gemma feel this way about him? Or was he fooling himself into thinking that she cared as much about him as he cared about her?

He had no idea and the uncertainty was the worst thing of all. He was used to being in charge of his life and his emotions and it wasn't easy to have all these question marks hanging over him.

Gemma had to climb quite a long way up the hill before she managed to get a signal on her phone. She dialled 999 and asked for the ambulance service then quickly explained what had happened. It was a relief when the operator assured her that an ambulance would be despatched immediately.

Leaving her phone switched on, she started to make her way back down to the road. The snow was falling so heavily now that she could see only a few inches in front of her, but so long as she kept going downhill, she reasoned, she should reach the road. The ground was extremely slippery, but she managed to remain upright until she reached a particularly steep part and her feet shot out from under her. She slithered down the hill on her back, stopping with a thud when she cannoned into an outcrop of rock.

It took her a moment to catch her breath and then she checked to see if she was injured. Apart from her left thigh, which was throbbing from coming into contact with the rocks, she seemed to be fine, thankfully enough. Scrambling to her feet, she tried to get her bearings, but she couldn't tell how close she was to the road. She couldn't even follow the slope of the land, either, because she'd landed in a hollow. She'd also dropped her phone, so even if by some lucky chance she could have got a signal, that was out of the question now. To all intents and purposes she was lost, and the best thing she could do was to take shelter and wait to be rescued.

Gemma damped down the panic that was welling up inside her as she huddled against the rocks. There was no need to be scared. Ross knew where she'd gone and when she didn't turn up at the surgery, he would alert the mountain rescue team…assuming he noticed she was missing, of course.

Her heart sank. After all, there was no reason why he should keep tabs on her. He may have kissed her but that didn't make him responsible for her. The fact that he hadn't mentioned what had happened on Sunday proved that he was keen to put it behind him, too. It had been a one-off, never-to-be-repeated experience, and it definitely wasn't a sign that he cared about her, if that was what she was hoping. Tears suddenly filled her eyes. She could be stuck out here for ages and nobody would miss her.

By nine o'clock, Ross was growing increasingly anxious. There was still no sign of Gemma, neither had there been a message from her to say why she had been delayed. He waited until his nine o'clock appointment left then phoned the nurses' room and spoke to Pam Whiteside, the other practice nurse.

'Any news from Gemma yet?'

'Nothing at all. It's just not like her not to let us know what's going on,' Pam added, sounding equally concerned.

'She was due to call at Naylor's Farm to take some bloods first thing this morning. Can you phone Jim Naylor and ask him if she's been there?'

Ross hung up after Pam agreed to make the call. He had a full list and couldn't afford to fall behind. He saw another patient then Pam phoned him back and confirmed that Gemma had been to the farm and had left there shortly after seven-thirty.

'I tried her mobile,' Pam told him. 'But it went straight through to voice mail. There's a number of places around here where you can't get a signal, but she should have been within range by now.'

'She certainly should. Thanks, Pam. I'll get back to you as soon as I hear something.'

Ross hung up and checked his watch. It was two hours since Gemma had left the farm. Although driving would be difficult in this weather, it shouldn't have taken her all this time to get back. He was more convinced than ever that something must have happened to her and, that being the case, the authorities needed to be informed.

The phone rang again and he snatched it up. It was Carol this time to tell him that the police had called to say that Gemma's car had been found by the side of the road, close to where an accident had happened. There was no sign of Gemma, although, according to Ambulance Control, it had been Gemma who had summoned assistance. The police had asked the mountain rescue team to organise a search party.

Ross felt physically sick as he thanked Carol and hung

up. He couldn't bear to think that Gemma was out on the hills in this weather. He knew that he wouldn't be able to concentrate until she was found so phoned through to Reception and told Dianne to hold back his next patient, then went to Matt's room and knocked on the door. Matt frowned in concern when Ross explained what had happened.

'She could be anywhere if she's wandered off and got lost.'

'I know. The police have alerted the mountain rescue team and I'd like to go along and help them, if that's OK with you. It will mean the rest of you having to pick up my appointments, though.'

'Not a problem,' Matt said immediately. 'We'll cover your workload. It's far more important that we find Gemma. You get yourself straight off.'

'Thanks. Can you ask Carol to let the mountain rescue team know that I'll meet them at their headquarters?'

'Will do. Take care, though. We don't want to lose two of our team in one day. It wouldn't do much for our reputation,' Matt added drily.

'It certainly wouldn't.' Ross summoned a smile, although there was a hollow feeling in his stomach. Maybe he was worrying unnecessarily, but he wouldn't rest until he found out where Gemma was.

He fetched his coat and left. He knew it would cause a stir because he had never left in the middle of surgery before, but some things were too important to put off, and this was one of them. He backed out of his parking space, feeling fear clawing at his insides when he saw the snow that was still falling on the hills. If Gemma was out there, they needed to find her as quickly as possible.

CHAPTER THIRTEEN

GEMMA made a determined effort to stop herself falling asleep. It wasn't easy because the snow was whirling around, covering everything with a thick layer of white that dazzled her eyes. She felt her eyelids drifting shut again and jerked herself awake. It was vital that she stay awake and try to keep warm. Thankfully, her coat had a thick thermal lining, but the cold was intense, seeping into her limbs and making them feel stiff and heavy.

She forced herself to her feet and flapped her arms like an injured bird attempting to take flight. Her feet were numb so she stamped up and down on the spot, wincing when her toes began to tingle. She'd been stuck there for over two hours and had no idea how much longer it would be before help arrived. Maybe she should try to find her way back to the road instead of waiting any longer?

She moved away from the shelter of the rocks, cautiously feeling her way forward as she didn't want to risk falling over again. The wind was extremely strong, buffeting her about as she inched her way across the uneven ground. She lost her footing and fell heavily, bruising her hip, but made herself get up and carry on. She had to get back to the road and find help.

Ross couldn't believe how cold it was. The wind was bitter, striking through the layers of clothing he was wearing, and he couldn't help worrying about Gemma. He was dressed for the weather but what had she been wearing when she had set off that morning?

'It looks like we may have a lead.' Max Jackson, leader of the mountain rescue team, came hurrying over and Ross swung round.

'Someone's seen her?'

'No, but we've managed to get the co-ordinates of where she was when she phoned for the ambulance.' Max spread an Ordnance survey map of the area across the bonnet of the Land Rover. 'The accident happened just here,' he explained, pointing to a section of the road. 'And the call came from here.' He placed his finger on a point halfway up one of the hills.

'She must have climbed up there to get a signal for her phone!' Ross exclaimed.

'It looks that way.' Max rolled up the map. 'My guess is that she lost her way when she was coming back down. It's easily done in this weather, but at least we have an idea where to start looking and that's something to be grateful for.'

Max didn't say anything else as they both climbed into the Land Rover. However, Ross was very aware that although they knew where to start the search, it wasn't going to be easy to find Gemma if she had wandered a long way off. He fastened his seat belt, feeling his nerves tighten as they began to drive further into the hills. The weather was atrocious here, great flurries of snow swirling across the countryside and making it extremely difficult to see where they were going. If Gemma was out there, he just didn't know how they were going to find her.

'We're going to use the dogs to track her,' Max informed him as they approached the crossroads. He made sure the road was clear before pulling out, checking in his rear-view mirror to make sure the rest of the vehicles were following. Ross knew that teams from neighbouring areas had been placed on standby in case they were needed as well. Although it was good to know that they could call on extra help, he couldn't bear to think it might be necessary if they failed to find Gemma themselves.

'Can the dogs follow a scent in these conditions?' he asked, trying to stay focussed. He would be no use if he started to panic and for Gemma's sake, he needed to be strong.

'Oh, yes. It's amazing what those dogs can sniff out,' Max assured him.

The conversation tailed off after that. Driving conditions were appalling and it needed complete concentration to keep them on the road. By the time they reached their destination, Ross was feeling desperate. He jumped out of the car as soon as they drew up, his heart racing when he saw Gemma's car parked at the side of the road. The other vehicles involved in the accident were in the process of being removed; the sports car had been loaded onto a trailer and the lorry was being winched back onto its wheels.

'We're going to head up to the spot from where she made that call,' Max informed him, and Ross took a steadying breath.

'So we can pick up her trail from there?'

'That's right.' Max glanced around to make sure the rest of the team were ready. The dog handler was crouched beside Gemma's car, letting the dogs get a good sniff at her scent. As soon as they were ready, he headed towards the lower reaches of the hill.

'Will there be a visible trail to follow?' Ross demanded as they all set off in pursuit.

'I doubt it. The snow's too heavy. It will have covered up any footprints.' He gave Ross a sympathetic look. 'The dogs are very good. If anyone can find her, they will.'

Ross had to be content with that but he couldn't deny that he was scared to death at how hit and miss it seemed. If the dogs failed to find Gemma's scent, he had no idea what they would do next. Panic reared up inside him again and once again he forced it down. He had to stay calm for Gemma's sake.

It seemed to take for ever before the dogs picked up a trail. Ross's nerves were at breaking point as they followed the animals. They reached an outcrop of rocks and the dogs milled around, barking excitedly, before setting off again. The scent was obviously stronger now which had to be a good sign, he hoped, but he had reached desperation point by the time the lead dog started barking and straining at its leash.

'There she is!' the dog handler shouted, pointing to a spot directly ahead of them.

Ross felt his heart surge into his throat when he saw the figure lying slumped on the ground. She looked so still, so lifeless, that he was afraid to move. Then all of a sudden, he was running towards her, slipping and sliding in his haste to reach her. He rolled her onto her back, placing his cheek to her mouth and feeling tears burn his eyes when he felt her breath on his skin. She was alive and that was a miracle in itself.

'Gemma, can you hear me? Sweetheart, it's Ross. Can you open your eyes for me?'

There was no response at first and then her lids slowly rose a fraction. 'Ross?'

'Thank God!' He pulled her into his arms, burying his face against her throat. It was only when he felt her shiver that he pulled himself together.

'We need to get you back to Dalverston, asap,' he said, standing up. The team had brought a stretcher with them and it took them only seconds to place Gemma on it and cover her with a heat-retaining blanket. Max radioed ahead with their location and arranged for them to be met on the road to save time, so once they had made their way down off the hill, Gemma was loaded into the back of the Land Rover.

'I'm going with her,' Ross informed them in a tone that brooked no argument. He climbed into the back, crouching down beside the stretcher. It wasn't the most comfortable position but he didn't give a damn. All he cared about was Gemma and making sure she was safe and well.

'How did you find me?' she whispered as they set off.

'The police managed to pinpoint where you made that phone call from,' he explained, smoothing back her damp hair. 'Once we knew exactly where you'd been, the dogs picked up your scent and followed your trail.'

'I feel so stupid. I can't believe I got lost like that.' She bit her lip and he saw her eyes fill with tears. 'I didn't think anyone would even notice I was missing, let alone come and look for me.'

'I noticed you were missing,' he said softly, wiping away a tear. 'I was worried sick when you didn't turn up for work and nobody knew where you were.'

'Were you?'

'Yes.' He wiped away another tear then smiled at her, uncaring what she might see in his eyes at that moment. He'd been through hell and just to have her here, safe and sound, was the best thing that had ever happened to him. 'I'll always worry about you, Gemma, because you're very important to me.'

He kissed her lightly on the forehead, hoping she understood what he was trying to say. Maybe it was too soon to tell her how he felt, but there was no point denying it. He loved her and the thought that he might have lost her today was more than he could bear. Now all he had to do was convince her that it was her he loved, and nobody else.

Gemma could feel her heart racing as she looked into Ross's eyes. There was something about the way he was looking at her that made her want to believe that he really cared about her. Surely he couldn't have looked at her with such tenderness and concern if she hadn't meant anything to him?

The Land Rover drew up outside A and E and the opportunity to ask him passed. Within seconds the stretcher was lifted out of the vehicle and placed on a trolley. The main doors whooshed open and the next minute she was being rushed along the corridor. It was like something that happened in one of those TV medical dramas—bright lights flashing overhead and people shouting instructions. It was all very surreal and a little scary, if she was honest.

'You're OK. There's nothing to worry about.'

All of a sudden Ross was beside her, gripping her hand as the convoy made its way to the treatment area. Gemma clung to him, needing him there beside her more than ever at that moment.

'So what have we here? My favourite practice nurse has been playing truant in the hills, I hear.'

Gemma looked round when she recognised Ben's voice and smiled shakily. 'Oh, it's you. Thank heavens for that. I thought I was in the middle of some sort of TV drama for a moment.'

'Who says you aren't?' Ben struck a pose. 'Picture this scene: handsome, brooding young medic saves the life of a pretty young nurse. During the course of his heroic treatment, she falls madly, deeply in love with the aforementioned medic and he with her. The last we see of them is the handsome medic wheeling her out of A and E on a trolley, at which point cue the violins.'

He hummed tunelessly as he pretended to play the violin. Gemma rolled her eyes. 'You need to get out more. It's obvious that you watch far too much television than is good for you.'

'Cruel woman. And here I was, trying to cheer you up.'

'You always did have a lousy bedside manner,' Ross said pithily, winking at her. 'That's one of the reasons why you're ideally suited to emergency work. Your patients don't stay long enough for you to bore them to death!'

'You two are ganging up on me now. Thanks. I'll remember this.'

Ben looked suitably wounded and Gemma chuckled. Their easy camaraderie was such a relief after all the stresses of the day. She looked up in surprise when Ross let go of her hand and moved away from the trolley.

'Although I have serious doubts about Ben's bedside manner, I have to admit he's pretty competent and doesn't need me supervising him.' He smiled into her eyes and she felt her breath catch when she saw the warmth in his gaze. 'I'll wait outside while he checks you over. OK?'

'Yes,' she whispered, feeling a little giddy because of what was happening. She drew in a shaky breath as Ross disappeared, doing her best to answer Ben's questions with a semblance of normality, although it wasn't easy when her mind was in such a spin.

Was she right in her assumptions that Ross cared about her? Everything pointed towards it yet she was afraid to believe it. Ross had loved Heather. He must still love her, too, because it was inconceivable that he could have changed his mind so quickly. And yet if that was the case, why had he looked at *her* as though she was the most important person in the world?

It was impossible to work it all out. In the end, Gemma gave up rather than risk driving herself mad. Thankfully, her injuries weren't serious. In fact, apart from a massive bruise on hip and another on her coccyx, she had come through the ordeal relatively unscathed. Ben told her to rest for the remainder of the day then had to rush off to attend to a patient who was far more seriously injured.

Gemma thanked the staff and went out to the waiting room, sighing when she saw Ross sitting near the door. She longed to believe that he cared about her but how could she? It was Heather he loved and Heather he'd wanted. He may have been worried about her, but to Ross she was simply a friend. She wasn't the woman he had hoped to spend his life with.

They took a taxi back to her house. Ross had insisted on seeing her home and Gemma hadn't had the heart to refuse. Maybe she was storing up more heartache for herself, but the need to be with him for a while longer was too strong to resist. Today of all days, she needed to feel as though someone cared about her.

The taxi drew up outside her house and she reached for the door handle. Although she hated to let him go, she knew that she had to be sensible. 'Thanks for seeing me home, Ross. I know you must be keen to get back to the surgery so I won't keep you.'

'I'm not going anywhere until I'm sure you're all right,' he said firmly. He paid the driver then joined her on the pavement, his brows arching when she made no move to let them into the house. 'Are we going to stand out here all day?'

'No, of course not.'

Gemma flushed as she dug her key out of her pocket. She let them in and went straight into the sitting room to poke up the fire. She added another log then put the guard around the grate. Ross was still standing by the door and there was the strangest expression on his face. He looked tense and on edge, and Gemma was suddenly struck by remorse for all the trouble she had caused him.

'I'm really sorry about what happened today. You have

enough to contend with at the moment without having to come looking for me.'

'Sorry?' he repeated in evident surprise. 'It wasn't your fault, Gemma. It was an accident. There's no need to apologise.'

'It's kind of you to say that, but if I'd been a bit more careful, I wouldn't have got lost.'

'You aren't to blame in any way, shape or form.' He came further into the room, his blue eyes boring into hers in a way that made her heart suddenly race as he stopped in front of her. 'You were trying to save those people's lives and you deserve a medal for what you did today—the way you put yourself at risk to help them.'

He touched her cheek, his fingers brushing so lightly across her skin that she should barely have registered it, yet all of sudden her body seemed to be on fire. Gemma gasped as a wave of heat flowed through her. Ross's eyes darkened, taking on the colour of a midnight sky as he stared into her face. When he pulled her into his arms, she didn't resist. Her breasts suddenly came into contact with his muscular chest and she sucked in her breath when she felt her nipples harden. She wanted him so much, wanted him and loved him too. And it was love that broke down the final barriers.

Winding her arms around his neck, she drew his head down and pressed her mouth to his. His lips were cool at first but they soon changed and she murmured in delight when she felt the heat of his mouth scorching hers. It felt as though Ross was branding her with his kiss, marking her as his property, and she gloried in the idea.

Opening her mouth, she invited him to deepen the kiss, uncaring how it would appear. She wanted him and she wasn't going to pretend otherwise. When his tongue slid into her mouth, she shuddered convulsively, feeling the hot sweet rush of desire that flowed through her. When Ross had kissed her before, he'd shown a certain restraint, but he wasn't holding anything back now. He kissed her hard and hungrily, arousing her passion as well as his own, so that they were both breathing heavily when he drew back, both needing a moment to find their way back down to earth.

He rested his forehead against hers and she felt the shudder that ran through him. 'I don't know what to say apart from wow.'

'Wow, indeed,' she repeated, shyly, and he chuckled as he pulled her to him again.

'You're not going all coy on me, I hope?'

'No-o-o…' She tailed off and he sighed as he tilted her face so that he could look into her eyes.

'It was a great kiss, Gemma, the *best* kiss I can remember. There's definitely nothing to be shy about.'

He kissed her again before she could reply and Gemma's head started to spin, a combination of the desire she was feeling and the shock of that declaration. How could it have been the best kiss Ross could remember? What about all those kisses he'd shared with Heather?

It was a puzzle of labyrinthine proportions and she simply wasn't up to solving it at that moment. Ross was kissing her again and again, showering her with the most wonderful kisses she had ever experienced too. She could feel herself drifting away on a tide of desire, her body aching for the fulfilment it so desperately wanted. Even when she felt his hands glide down the sides of her breasts, she wasn't alarmed. She needed him to touch her, caress her, show her how much he wanted her.

He rubbed his thumbs over her nipples and she shuddered. When he bent and nuzzled her breasts through the fabric of her dress, she moaned. She could imagine how wonderful it would feel if he kissed her there without anything in the way…

His hand went to the zip that ran down the front of her dress and all of a sudden sanity returned, icily cold and doubly scary because she'd allowed herself to forget. She couldn't let Ross make love to her. She didn't dare. He would take one look at her damaged body and be disgusted by what he saw.

For a moment fear locked her throat so that she couldn't ask him to stop. All she could think of was the fact that she couldn't bear it if Ross looked at her with revulsion!

CHAPTER FOURTEEN

Ross inched the zip down the merest fraction then paused, Gemma's rigid posture warning him that something wasn't right. His heart spasmed with fear when he saw the expression on her face. She looked scared to death all of a sudden and he had no idea why.

'Gemma? Sweetheart, what is it? What's wrong?'

He cupped her face between his hands, feeling the tremor that passed through her, although he knew it wasn't desire that had caused it this time. He had seen the effect desire could have on her and this was in no way similar to that. His body made its own very emphatic statement as he recalled how she'd looked a few moments earlier but he forced it to behave. This wasn't the time to lose control, not when something was so badly wrong.

'Gemma, talk to me. Tell me what's wrong,' he pleaded, desperate to get through to her and he did, although her reaction wasn't what he had expected.

'I'm sorry but I think you should leave.' She pulled herself out of his arms, her back ramrod straight, her head held high—a posture that smacked of rejection.

Ross was in no doubt that she really did want him to go.

He'd have needed to be clueless not to have worked that out. However, what he didn't understand was why she had gone from wanting him to rejecting him in the blink of an eye. He regarded her levelly, determined that he was going to get to the root of this puzzle.

'This seems to have been an extremely rapid change of heart. Did I do something wrong, Gemma? Because if I did, I'd much prefer it if you told me what it was.'

'It's got nothing to do with you,' she said shortly, walking to the door. It was obvious that she wanted him to leave but Ross had no intention of going until he knew what had happened.

'How can it have nothing to do with me? One minute we're just a step away from going to bed together, and the next moment you're throwing me out on my ear. It's a little difficult *not* to take it personally, I'm afraid.'

Colour rushed to her face but she met his eyes. 'I apologise if you think I was leading you on.'

'Tsk! We were leading each other on, Gemma.' He grasped her hands, feeling even more concerned when he discovered how cold they were. 'There was nothing one-sided about what happened—we were in it together!'

Her lower lip wobbled but she managed to hold on to her composure. 'Maybe we were, but that doesn't make it right.'

'Doesn't it?'

Ross stared at her as he tried to understand what she was saying. It was hard to get a fix on the real meaning because the sight of her mouth quivering like that was playing havoc with his ability to reason…

Not right equalled wrong, a small voice whispered. Gemma thought they'd been wrong to start kissing and that it definitely would have been wrong for them to make love. But why?

The cogs inside his brain were whirring now and Ross gasped as he realised what was behind her sudden withdrawal. Gemma thought it would be wrong to make love to him because of Heather! He gripped her hands, desperate to convince her there was nothing to fear.

'If you stopped because you feel guilty about Heather, there's no need. Heather doesn't love me—she proved that by calling off our wedding. And, more importantly, I don't love her and I never did.' His voice dropped as emotion got the better of him. 'I never felt this way about Heather, I swear.'

Tears filled her eyes as she looked up at him. 'You may think that now, but you'll change your mind, Ross.'

'I won't. I know how I feel and I've never felt this strongly about anyone before.'

She was shaking her head before he had finished speaking. 'You mustn't say that, Ross, please. I don't want to hear it.'

'Why not?' He gripped her hands so tightly that he felt her wince and forced himself to relax his grip. 'There's nothing to stop us being together if it's what we both want, Gemma. I know it all seems very sudden, and that you might be worried that I'm on the rebound, but I promise you that isn't the case. I really care about you. I lo—'

'No!' She dragged her hands free and stepped back, her face paper-white, her eyes swimming with tears. 'I'm sorry, Ross, but I want you to leave now.'

Ross felt a tearing pain rip through his guts. He couldn't believe that she was rejecting him but he only needed to see the expression on her face to know that she wouldn't change her mind. Swinging round, he strode out of the room and wrenched open the front door, wondering how he was going to bear it. He loved her so much but she didn't want him. His heart felt as though it was shattering into hundreds of tiny pieces.

'I'm sorry, Ross. Really I am.'

He glanced back, feeling the pain inside him intensify when he saw the anguish on her face. He might be hurting but Gemma was hurting too, and that thought was too much to bear. The least he could do was absolve her of any guilt she might feel for rejecting him.

'There's no need to apologise. Maybe you're right. It's been that sort of day when emotions run unnaturally high.' He managed to smile but it cost him dearly. 'I'm sure we'll both look back on what's happened and wonder how one thing led to another.'

She reared back as though he had slapped her. 'Then let's be grateful that we called a halt when we did.'

'Indeed.' He glanced at his watch. 'I'd better get back to work before Matt thinks I've gone AWOL. I'll see you tomorrow.'

Another quick smile and he was out of the door. There was a taxi dropping off a fare so he flagged it down and asked the driver to take him to the surgery. He knew Gemma was watching but he didn't look back. He didn't dare. If he looked back, he would have to go back and tell her that he had lied, that he loved her and wanted to spend his life making her happy, and it wasn't what she wanted to hear.

The truth was that Gemma neither loved nor wanted him and he had to accept that and not embarrass her by causing a scene. He should be used to it by now because it wasn't the first time he'd been rejected, only this time it really hurt. This time he had lost the woman he truly loved with all his heart.

The days rushed by, turned into weeks, Christmas and New Year came and went. Gemma spent the holiday in Leeds with her parents, fielding their questions about why she was so quiet. She couldn't tell them about Ross or why her heart was broken. They had suffered enough after her accident and it wouldn't be fair to upset them again by explaining how it had affected her life. Her parents thought she had put it behind her and she preferred to let them believe that rather than tell them the truth.

She returned to work both desperate to see Ross and dreading it. He'd been so distant towards her since that day he had rescued her from the hills that she had found herself avoiding him. However, she knew that if they were to continue working together, she had to find a way to deal with what had happened.

Her first morning back was frantically busy. The surgery was packed after the extended break. Gemma saw patients non-stop all morning long then had another hectic session in the afternoon at the mother-and-baby clinic. Fortunately, Fraser Kennedy, their locum, was taking it that day so she was able to relax. However, shortly before they were due to finish, one of the mums who had been waiting her turn came rushing into the room.

'It's Abigail. I can't wake her up!' she cried, thrusting the little girl into Gemma's arms.

'Put her on the couch,' Fraser instructed.

Gemma laid the infant down and unzipped her jacket.

The poor little mite was waxy pale and there was a thin blue line around her mouth. Fraser took one look at the child and tipped back her head.

'Get Ross in here,' he ordered, placing his mouth over the little one's nose and mouth as he started to breathe for her.

Gemma didn't hesitate. She ran out of the room and along the corridor, bursting into Ross's room without bothering to knock. 'Can you come? We've got a ten-month-old baby who's stopped breathing.'

'Do we know what happened?' he demanded, leaping up from his desk.

'No. Mum was too distraught to tell us.' Gemma ran back to the clinic room with Ross hard on her heels. He immediately took stock of the scene as he hurried over to join Fraser.

'I'll take over the breathing,' he informed the younger man, then turned to Gemma. 'We need an ambulance, asap. Once you've sorted that out, see what you can get out of the mother. We need to know exactly what we're dealing with.'

'Will do.'

Gemma hurriedly phoned for an ambulance. Abigail's mother, Amanda Thomas, was standing by the wall, shaking uncontrollably. Gemma gently urged her to a chair and sat her down.

'Can you tell me what happened? Is it possible that Abigail swallowed something—a sweet perhaps?'

'No, no, nothing like that. She just went sort of…*stiff* and I couldn't rouse her.' Her breath caught on a sob. 'Please don't let her die, I beg you.'

'The doctors are doing everything possible for her,'

Gemma assured her. She took hold of Amanda's hand, knowing how vital it was to find out what had happened to the child. 'Has Abigail been ill recently?'

'She's had a bit of a cold for the past few days. I thought she was teething—she tends to get the snuffles when she cuts a tooth. But last night she felt really hot and she was very fretful, too…'

Amanda tailed off, her eyes welling with tears as she watched Ross and Fraser working on her daughter. Gemma squeezed her hand to regain her attention.

'Was that all? There was just a fever? You didn't notice a rash on her?'

'No, nothing… Oh, apart from a sort of bruise in the crook of her elbow. I don't know how that happened.'

'I'll tell the doctors what you've told me.'

Gemma hurried over to the couch. 'Mum says the baby had a temperature last night. She's been off colour for a few days—snuffly and very fretful—but Mum thought she might have been teething. She didn't notice a rash but, apparently, there's a bruise in the crook of Abigail's elbow and she has no idea how it happened.'

'Which arm?' Ross demanded, looking up.

'I'll check.' Gemma hurried back to Amanda and found out the information then went back. 'Her right arm. I'll snip open her sleeve.'

She quickly cut through the little girl's sweater with a pair of blunt-ended scissors, frowning when she saw the strange purplish mark in the bend of the child's arm. 'How odd!' she exclaimed.

'I need intravenous antibiotics, stat!' Ross rapped out in between breaths. He paused while Fraser checked the baby's pulse and Gemma felt relief run through her when the locum announced that Abigail now had a much stronger pulse and that she was breathing on her own.

'We'll give her oxygen,' Ross told the younger doctor. 'You set that up while Gemma sorts out the antibiotics.'

He rattled out the dosage then turned back to the child, leaving Gemma wondering why the bruise was so significant. There was no time to ask him, though. She drew up the requested antibiotics then helped Ross administer them, cradling the little girl while the injection was given. Fraser had fetched the oxygen tank and, following Ross's instructions, set the dial to deliver the requisite flow. Too much would damage the baby's lungs while too little wouldn't have the desired effect.

By the time that was done, the ambulance had arrived. One of the paramedics carried Abigail out and Gemma hurriedly ushered Amanda after them. She gave the woman a hug, wishing there was something more she could do. As a single mum, Amanda would have to go through this ordeal on her own and it was upsetting to think how hard it must be for her.

'I'm sure she'll be all right,' Fraser said, noticing Gemma's downcast expression as they headed back inside. 'Ross knows what he's doing and I'm sure he's covered all the bases.'

'Yes, of course.' Gemma summoned a smile then went to her room and sat down. She couldn't bear to think that poor little Abigail might not pull through after all their efforts.

'She has a good chance of recovering from this,' a voice said from the doorway and she looked up to find Ross watching her.

'Do you think so?' she muttered wearily.

'Yes. The antibiotics should be kicking in even as we speak.' He came further into the room although he didn't close the door. Was he making sure that this highly emotive situation wouldn't trigger another unwanted rush of passion? she wondered sickly. Maybe she had been the one to call a halt previously, but Ross had accepted her decision without too much protest.

'What was so significant about that bruise on Abigail's arm?' she asked sharply because the thought hurt.

'It could be an indication of bacterial meningitis—I've seen it once before. A child was admitted to A and E while I was doing my rotation there complaining of a fever and there was a bruise on his inner arm too. There were no other symptoms—no sensitivity to light, no stiffness in the neck, no headache, just the bruise and an elevated temperature.' He shrugged. 'I was on the point of sending him home with a script for paracetamol when the consultant happened to pass the cubicle.'

'And he told you it was meningitis?' Gemma said, interested despite herself.

'He did. He wiped the floor with me, in fact, although only *after* he'd given the boy intravenous antibiotics and sent him up to PICU.' He smiled wryly. 'It taught me a valuable lesson, though, and that was never to disregard anything out of the ordinary, no matter how insignificant it may appear. It was worth getting a rollicking just for that.'

'Especially if it's helped to save little Abigail's life now,' she agreed quietly.

'Exactly.'

Ross went on his way and Gemma got down to work.

There was a pile of paperwork that needed her attention but she couldn't seem to settle to it. The fact that Ross had shared that story with her had touched her deeply. Although he was always willing to offer guidance, it was rare that he spoke about his own experiences like that. It made her see that he had changed in the past few weeks, become more open and giving, and it made her love him more than ever.

He was such a wonderful doctor and such a good man, steady and reliable, trustworthy and honest. Admitting that to herself made his recent behaviour all the more puzzling, too. He had told her that he wasn't in love with Heather and she couldn't believe that he would have lied to her about something so important. Maybe he had blamed their heightened emotions for them nearly ending up in bed together, but she couldn't imagine Ross allowing himself to get carried away under any circumstances. It was far more likely he had told her that to stop her feeling guilty about rejecting him.

It was a painful thought. Even though Gemma knew she'd had no choice but to call a halt, it wasn't easy to accept that she might have rejected Ross's love. To be loved by him was the one thing she had always dreamed of. However, even though it broke her heart to know that she had lost her chance of finding true happiness, it didn't change things. She still couldn't bear the thought of him seeing her scars and being repulsed by them. She would rather suffer the heartache of losing him than go through that nightmare.

Ross was somewhat surprised he had told Gemma that story. He rarely spoke about himself, yet he'd felt a need to share it with her when he'd seen how upset she'd been. The past few weeks had changed him, and more and more he had found himself opening up. He no longer felt that he needed to hold back, and it was all because of the way he felt about Gemma. He loved her with his whole heart and that had helped him tap into his emotions in a way he'd been afraid to do before. However, he mustn't forget that Gemma had made it clear she didn't want him. He wouldn't embarrass her by being too open about his feelings again.

Fortunately, evening surgery was as busy as the morning one had been so there was no time to brood. Before he knew it, it was time to go home. Matt popped his head round the door as Ross was getting ready to leave.

'I'm having a few people round on Saturday night—a sort of late New Year's party. There wasn't time to organise anything before Christmas with one thing and another, so this is my way of making up for it. I hope you'll come, Ross?'

'Oh, right. Thanks.' Ross wasn't sure what to say. He still felt a little guilty whenever he thought of how Matt had suffered over the wedding.

'Look, Ross, I know you feel awkward because of what happened between you and Heather, but there's no need. It was Heather's decision to cancel the wedding and I accept that. You're part of this practice and a very valuable part, too.' Matt shrugged. 'What I'm trying to say is that I don't want it to affect our working relationship.'

Ross was deeply touched. 'Thank you. That means a lot to me, Matt.'

'Then I'll take that as a yes and expect you on Saturday.'

Ross felt his spirits lift as he collected his coat. It was

good to know that Matt didn't hold him solely responsible for what had happened. Although he had been partly to blame, maybe it hadn't been all down to him. Maybe Heather had had her own agenda for marrying him and had realised at the last minute that she'd been making a mistake.

It was the first time he had considered that idea, and the more he thought about it, the more sense it made. Heather hadn't been wildly in love with him any more than he'd been wildly in love with her. She'd agreed to marry him because he'd suited her requirements. And that being the case, he no longer needed to keep blaming himself for what had happened. Hallelujah!

There was a definite spring in his step as he went into the office. Gemma was in there and his upbeat mood rapidly dissipated when he saw how she avoided looking at him. He sighed as he dropped his files into the tray and bade everyone goodnight. He may have cleared his conscience where Heather was concerned, but it appeared he had caused Gemma a lot of problems. If only he could find a way to make it up to her, but how could he when she wouldn't let him near her? He would never have kissed her if he'd known the damage it would cause...

He groaned. Like hell he wouldn't! The moment he'd had her in his arms, he'd been lost. Not that she'd been exactly reluctant, had she? She'd definitely met him halfway, returned his passion with an enthusiasm which made him go hot all over as he recalled it now. Whatever had made her call a halt, it hadn't been a lack of interest. Gemma had wanted him so what had made her change her mind?

Ross puzzled over the question for the rest of the night but he had no idea what the answer was. Only Gemma knew and he was very much afraid that she wasn't going to tell him. The thought that he might lose her and never know why was too much to bear. Ross realised that he had to make her explain, although he had no idea how he would go about it. Hopefully, inspiration would strike him soon.

CHAPTER FIFTEEN

GEMMA really didn't want to go to the party but she simply couldn't think of an excuse. All the staff were going and it would look very odd if she didn't turn up. In the end she accepted that she would have to go. After all, it wasn't as though Ross would care one way or the other if she was there.

The thought hurt unbearably, but she was determined not to let anyone know how she felt. She took her time getting ready, opting to wear a new dress her mother had bought her for Christmas. Made from sumptuous red velvet, it was simply cut with long sleeves and a straight skirt that ended just above her knees. From the front the dress was positively demure, but from the back it was a different story entirely. Gemma had been a little shocked when she'd seen it. However, at her mother's urging she had tried it on and discovered how flattering it was. The low-cut back showed off the slender line of her spine to advantage, while the ruby-red colour highlighted her porcelain-pale skin.

Pleased with the reflection she could see in the mirror that evening, she decided to hype up the image of sophistication and pinned her hair into a loose knot that exposed the nape of her neck. A little more make-up than usual also helped to create the illusion of a woman in control. So long as nobody looked beneath the surface veneer, she should be fine.

The party was in full swing by the time Gemma arrived. Rachel was acting as Matt's hostess and she greeted Gemma warmly.

'Come in. I'm so glad you were able to make it… Oh, don't you look gorgeous! That dress really suits you, doesn't it, Ross?'

Gemma's breath caught when she glanced round and saw Ross standing behind her. He looked so handsome in a well-cut black suit and a midnight-blue shirt that her senses immediately started to spin. It took a massive effort to smile at him as though nothing was amiss.

'Hello, Ross. How are you?'

'Fine, thank you.' He turned to his mother but not before Gemma had seen the oddest expression cross his face, a kind of wistful longing that made her pulse race. 'You're right. Gemma looks really lovely tonight.'

Somehow Gemma managed to keep her smile in place as she excused herself and went to find the others. Everyone had congregated in the kitchen where the drinks were being served and they greeted her with a cheer.

'Took your time, didn't you?' Carol piped up, handing her a glass of wine. 'Although I can see why you decided to make an entrance. That dress is fab!'

'Thank you kindly.' Gemma gave Carol a twirl, grinning when her friend whistled as she caught sight of her back. 'Mum bought it for me for Christmas. You don't think it's too much, do you?'

'By too much I suppose you mean too sexy?' Carol retorted. 'Definitely not. If you've got it, flaunt it!'

Gemma chuckled. Away from the surgery, Carol was a lot of fun and she always enjoyed spending time with her. They chatted about inconsequentials after that—how busy it had been at work, Carol's teenage daughter, Holly, who was dating her first boyfriend. Other people joined in, the conversation flowing as they moved into the sitting room. More guests were arriving all the time so that the house was soon packed with people having a good time, although Gemma couldn't help noticing that Ross didn't seem to be enjoying himself. He looked very strained and it bothered her to see him looking that way even though she knew there was nothing she could do about it.

By the time Matt announced the buffet was being served in the dining room, Gemma was desperate to leave. She let the others go on ahead, wondering if she could slip away without them noticing. The last of their group left the sitting room and she was about to make a hasty exit when she realised that Ross was still there. Heat flowed through her when she saw the way he was looking at her. She had no idea what it meant but all of a sudden she knew that she had to avoid a confrontation at all costs.

'Thinking of leaving so soon?' he said softly as he crossed the room.

'I...I've got a headache,' she said quickly, moving towards the door.

'Really?' He stepped in front of her so that she was forced to stop. 'It's come on rather suddenly, hasn't it?'

'It's been threatening all day,' she retorted, trying to step around him, but once again he barred her way.

'Come on, Gemma, why lie? You haven't got a head-ache, you just want to leave.'

'And what if I do?' she replied, glaring at him. 'You're not my keeper, Ross. If I choose to leave, it's my business.'

'Of course it is, unless you're leaving because of me.' He caught her hands. 'You're running away because you can't bear to be in the same room as me, aren't you, Gemma? Yet you didn't feel this way the other week. You were happy to be with me then. In fact, I'd go so far as to say that you wanted to be very close to me indeed.'

He pulled her to him until she was resting against him. Gemma felt a rush of sensations spill through her as she felt her breasts flatten against the wall of his chest. She closed her eyes as a wave of longing washed over her. How she had yearned for this moment, ached to lean on him and let him take away all the pain. To know that Ross loved her, wanted her, desired her, would make up for all the long years of loneliness. She would feel whole again, perfect, a woman fit to be loved. The woman Ross loved.

Thoughts tumbled round inside her head, so tempting, so beguiling, that she almost let herself believe it could happen. And then she felt Ross's hand glide down the smooth bare skin of her spine, felt his fingers slide inside the soft, warm velvet, sensed them hovering above the one part of her body no man would ever want to touch, and she knew in that instant that she couldn't bear it, couldn't stand to have him touch her there and feel the ugly, puckered flesh.

'No!' She pushed him away and ran from the room, uncaring what people thought as she fled past them and along the hall. Her car was parked outside and she climbed in, her hands shaking so that she could barely fit the key into the ignition. She managed it at last and thrust the car into gear, pulling away with a squeal of tyres. She had a last glimpse of Ross's shocked face as he followed her out to the drive and then she was turning into the road, leaving him behind where he must remain. There was no future for her and Ross, no future for her, a woman whose body was damaged beyond repair.

For a full minute Ross stood exactly where he was, transfixed with shock. He couldn't believe what had happened, the way Gemma had run from him in such terror...

His heart contracted as he recalled the anguish on her face when she had pushed him away. He had no idea what he had done to cause such a reaction, but he intended to find out. No way was he going to let this go. No way was he going to let Gemma go. He loved her and one way or another he was going to tell her that!

He ran out to his car and got in. Fortunately, the traffic had returned to normal now that the festivities were over so it didn't take him long to drive to Gemma's house. Her car was parked outside and there was a light on in the sitting room, which were encouraging signs, not that he would have cared if the place had been in darkness. He was going to have this out with her and if it took all night then it was just too bad.

It took half a dozen thumps with the door knocker before Gemma opened the door. Ross's heart turned over when he saw her tear-streaked face. He couldn't bear to think that he was the cause of her distress when he loved her so much.

'I'm so sorry, my love. I never meant to hurt you, but I

need to know what's going on.' He paused, but she didn't say anything, didn't invite him in or tell him to leave. She just stood there, looking as though the world had crashed down around her, and he couldn't bear it a moment longer.

Taking hold of her by the shoulders, he gently turned her round and ushered her inside. Normally, he wouldn't have imposed himself on her like this, but this wasn't a normal situation. Desperate times called for desperate measures and he was prepared to do anything it took to resolve this problem, whatever it was.

'Come and sit down.'

He sat her down on the sofa, picking up one of the throws and wrapping it around her when he saw her shiver. The fire had died down so he added a couple of logs, and still Gemma didn't say anything. Crouching down in front of her, he took hold of her hands.

'I don't know what's wrong, sweetheart, but whatever it is, we can work it out. I promise you that.'

'No,' she whispered, raising tear-drenched eyes to his face. 'There's nothing you can do, Ross. There's nothing anyone can do.'

Her voice broke on a sob and he couldn't stand it. Pulling her into his arms, he held her close, cradling her against his heart because it was the one place she needed to be at the moment. If he could make her understand how much he loved her, then nothing else mattered.

She let him hold her for a few minutes then drew back. 'I think you should leave now. I know you mean to be kind…'

He swore roughly then apologised. 'I'm sorry, but being kind isn't my main concern at this minute. I want to know why you're upset and why you ran away just now.' He cradled her face between his hands. 'I love you, Gemma, and I think you love me, too. That's why I'm not going to let you fob me off any longer. I want the truth, Gemma. Please.'

Her eyes closed for a moment before they opened again and he saw the despair they held. 'If it's the only way I can make you understand how pointless this is then I don't have a choice.'

She stood up, taking him by surprise so that he had no time to stop her. However, instead of walking out of the room, as he'd expected her to do, she moved to the very centre and stopped. Ross's breath caught when he saw her hands go to the zip at the side of her dress. He had no idea what was going on but he didn't move a muscle as she slid the zipper down its runner. Gemma didn't look at him as she let it fall to the floor in a soft heap. All she had on now was a red lace bra and matching panties and his blood pressure zoomed several notches up the scale as he took stock of her beautiful body, all the dips and curves, the softness, the silky fine skin…

She suddenly turned around and he couldn't stem the gasp that escaped his lips when he saw the ridges of scar tissue that marred the left side of her body. There wasn't just one scar but dozens, criss-crossing each other and forming a network. Some were obviously the scars left by surgery, others were the result of some kind of terrible accident, not that it mattered what had caused them. The fact that they were there, and that Gemma thought they were of such significance, was what really hurt him.

He stood up and walked towards her, feeling his love for her filling every cell in his body. He knew how much she must have suffered over the years, suspected that he knew why too.

Had some man seen these scars and been repulsed by them? he wondered, and knew it was true. The thought tipped him over the edge. To imagine how Gemma—this beautiful, tender-hearted woman—must have suffered was too much.

He dropped to his knees in front of her and let his fingers trace the raw, red network of tissue, feeling her flinch when he touched it. The biggest scar could only have been caused by major surgery and his heart shuddered with fear at the thought that he might have lost her before he'd had the chance to fall in love with her.

'They had to take away my kidney and my spleen,' she informed him in a tight little voice that echoed with pain.

'The surgeon did a first-rate job,' he murmured, leaning forward so that his lips could caress the red line that scored her skin.

Gemma shivered, her hand moving automatically to his head, although whether to push him away or hold him there he wasn't sure. He didn't give her time to make up her mind as his fingers moved on, following the trail as it spread around her body.

'Those were caused by the metal cutting into me,' she said with a wobble in her voice. 'The other car rammed into the side of us and bits of the door sliced into me.'

Ross winced as the scene played itself out in his head. He forced it away as he let his lips delicately trace the cobweb of red, from the front of her body round to the base of her spine. There was a puckered patch there too, just an inch or so above her buttocks, but he was less conscious of that than he was of the soft curve of her hips, the rounded swell of her bottom, the creamy tops of her thighs…

He breathed deeply then pressed his mouth to the spot,

let it linger, let his tongue touch it, taste it, heal it and, hopefully, her. She might have these scars but they meant nothing to him apart from the fact that they had caused her to suffer: for that reason alone he hated them but not for any other. They certainly didn't detract from her beauty, they enhanced it. They were proof of her courage, her will to survive against the greatest of odds. They summed up everything Gemma was—a beautiful, loving, strong and caring woman any man would be proud to love.

Ross let his mouth carry on exploring—across her spine, over the dip of her waist, round to her tummy, her navel… He groaned as his tongue slid into the dip of her belly button. He could have let it remain there for a lifetime only there were more delights to explore, not to mention the fact that his knees were in danger of seizing up. He staggered to his feet and grimaced.

'I'll have to give up skiing,' he muttered, seeing her eyes widen at the non sequitur. He grinned ruefully. 'I don't want the old knees to give up the ghost at an inopportune moment, do I?'

'But what about these?' She glanced down at herself then looked away as though she couldn't bear to see her own flesh.

'What about them?' He dropped a kiss on her mouth then another on the tip of her nose for no other reason than he wanted to. 'If you imagine they're going to put me off then think again. I love you and it doesn't matter to me how many scars you have.'

'But they're so ugly, so…so repulsive…' She tailed off and he sighed.

'Did someone tell you that, my darling?'

'Yes. The first and only man I ever slept with.' She tilted

her head, a hint of challenge in her eyes. 'After that, I swore I wouldn't put myself through that kind of pressure again.'

'Whoever he was, he was a fool,' he said roughly, pulling her to him. He felt the rigidity of her body but he didn't let it deter him. She wanted him, he could tell. She was just afraid of being hurt and he understood that feeling only too well.

His lips stroked across hers, nibbling, tasting, and he felt her relax a little and smiled. When he let his mouth trail kisses up her cheek and across her brow, he heard her murmur, tiny little sounds of pleasure that spurred him on. He was going to make this night so special that she would forget all about what had gone on before.

The thought immediately set light to his ardour as he pulled her to him and kissed her with a hunger he couldn't disguise. The magical thing was that Gemma kissed him back, her lips as eager as his were. When he reached around to unhook her bra, she helped him, dispensing with the tricky little clasp far quicker than he could have done. Her panties came next and then she was standing in front of him, naked and beautiful.

'You are so beautiful,' he said, mesmerised by the sight of her pale skin, her curves, her femininity. He ran his palms down her sides, from breast to thigh, and shuddered at the desire it aroused in him to touch her like that. When her hands went to his shirt as she began to undress him, he didn't move a muscle. He couldn't. He was transfixed with longing, with need, with love. It was only when her hands touched the buckle on his belt that he snapped out of his trance.

'Let's make ourselves a little more comfortable,' he murmured, lifting her into his arms and carrying her over to the sofa. He laid her down on the cushions then had to pause while he mustered a bit of self-control for the next bit.

'Ross?'

A hint of fear coloured her voice and he realised with a rush of tenderness that she had misconstrued his hesitation. He smiled wryly as he knelt beside her. 'Just taking a breather in case I got too excited. Where's that legendary control of mine when I need it most?'

She laughed softly, her cheeks filling with rosy colour. 'You could try a couple of deep breaths.'

'I just tried that. Take it from me, it hasn't worked!'

He bent and kissed her, letting his tongue slide between her lips, feeling their passion soar out of control. It took him just seconds to shed his own clothes so that he was lying naked beside her. Bending, he kissed her breasts, stroked her nipples, aroused her and himself to the point where there was no hope of holding back, not that either of them wanted to. When he entered her, she was ready for him, welcomed him, loved him with her body as well as with her mind.

Their love-making was the most profound experience Ross had ever had. He'd never believed it was possible to feel so close to someone, to know that every beat of her heart made his heart beat too; that her every breath was precious to him as well. In that moment he knew that real love, the love he felt for Gemma and she felt for him, had changed him for ever. He had found himself in her arms, discovered who he was and who he wanted to be and that, quite simply, was the man Gemma loved.

CHAPTER SIXTEEN

ALTHOUGH they didn't tell anyone about their new relationship, it wasn't long before the staff at the surgery guessed that something was going on. It caused a bit of a stir at first, but Gemma didn't care. She was so gloriously happy that nothing could dampen her mood, especially when Ross had made it clear that he felt the same way.

Once everyone got over their initial surprise, they were delighted for them. The only person Gemma was concerned about was Matt. She had no idea how he would react when he found out that she and Ross were a couple, but she needn't have worried. He seemed genuinely pleased when they told him, and there was no doubting his sincerity when he offered them his good wishes for the future.

It seemed to put the seal on their happiness. Not only were they working together, they were living together too. They spent their nights at Gemma's house because Ross preferred it to his own home. And every second of every hour they spent together made Gemma love him even more.

As for their love-making, it could only be described as perfect. For the first couple of weeks, she had found herself unconsciously watching him, half-afraid that her scars might repulse him in some way. However, it had soon become clear that Ross didn't see them as imperfections. He accepted them and they certainly didn't have any bearing on how much he loved her—that was obvious. Knowing that restored her confidence in herself as a woman. Gemma no longer saw herself as damaged goods but as a woman with a wonderful future ahead of her. Although they hadn't made any plans, she knew that one day she and Ross would get married and have that family she had dreamed of.

When Matt telephoned one Friday night to tell Ross that Heather was home for a visit, it didn't worry her the way it once would have done. She knew that Ross loved her and that she had nothing to fear. To her mind she was the luckiest woman alive and she told him that later that evening as they were making love.

'It's me who's the lucky one,' he said, looking into her eyes. 'The thought that I could have gone through my life and not experienced this kind of happiness scares me to death.' He kissed her hungrily. 'You've given me so much joy, Gemma. I don't know how to thank you.'

'And you've given me back my confidence,' she whispered against his mouth. 'I never thought I was capable of being loved but you've shown me that I was wrong.' She bit gently at his lower lip, feeling the shudder than ran through his powerful frame and glorying in the effect she had on him. 'I think that makes us quits, Ross, don't you?'

'Mmm…'

The rest of the sentence was swallowed up as he kissed her with a passion that made talking unnecessary. Their love-making seemed to reach new heights that night, forging an even stronger bond between them, one they both knew could never be broken. As she drifted off to sleep in his arms, Gemma knew that she couldn't be happier. She had the man she loved with all her heart lying beside her and a future filled with love ahead of her. Ross was everything she had ever wanted, and the best thing was that she was everything he wanted too.

Ross awoke early the next morning despite the fact that he and Gemma hadn't fallen asleep until the early hours. He smiled as he propped himself up on his elbow and watched her sleeping. Her lips were slightly parted, inviting his kiss, but he managed to resist the temptation. She needed her rest after their night of passion. His body made its own, very predictable statement about that thought and he grinned as he climbed out of bed. A cold shower was called for if he was to stick to his decision to let Gemma catch up on her sleep.

Fifteen minutes later, showered and dressed and having consumed a cup of coffee to warm him up, he set off for a walk. It was still early and there were few people about as he made his way to the river. He walked as far as the weir then turned back, wanting to be there when Gemma woke up. She should have had enough rest by then, he thought, lengthening his stride at the prospect of a little more *intimate* exercise. He rounded a bend in the path and ground to a halt when he saw the woman walking towards him. What on earth was Heather doing here at this hour of the morning?

Gemma was in the kitchen making a pot of tea when she heard Ross come in. 'I'm in here,' she called, dropping teabags into the pot.

'Hmm, now, that's a sight to gladden a man's heart.' He came up behind her, rubbing his cold cheek against her warm one as he pulled her into his arms.

'You're freezing!' she squealed, struggling rather ineffectually to free herself.

'But I'll soon warm up,' he assured her, smiling lasciviously as he trickled icy-cold kisses down her neck.

Gemma shivered and not just because of the chill of his lips. The feel of his mouth was playing havoc with her self-control. She gasped when he pulled her back against him and she felt his erection pressing against her buttocks. Obviously, it was having an effect on Ross as well!

He turned her round and kissed her properly, his mouth hot and hungry now as it demanded a response she was only too eager to give him. All she had on was the over-sized T-shirt she had slept in and that was soon dispensed with. Gemma gasped when he lifted her up so that her legs were wrapped around his hips. Her back was pressed against the kitchen cupboard and the feel of the solid wood against her spine and Ross's heat and hardness against her front was a potent combination.

He made love to her right there in the kitchen, calling out her name as he climaxed. Gemma clung to him as they both rode out the storm, feeling their passion melting her bones. She loved him so much, wanted him even more. He was her world, her life, her love, and the thought brought tears to her eyes which he kissed away.

'I'm not really crying,' she murmured. 'I'm just so happy.'

'Me too.' He kissed her softly and with great tenderness then picked up her T-shirt and gently pulled it over her head. 'You get back into bed and I'll bring you a cup of tea.'

'Give me five minutes to have a shower,' she begged him, and he grinned at her.

'Just five. If you take longer than that, I'm coming to get you out.'

'Promises, promises,' she retorted, skipping smartly out of the way when he made a grab for her. She raced up the stairs, smiling as she headed into the bathroom. She loved it when he teased her like that, loved it when he didn't too. In fact, she loved him whatever he did!

Ross was waiting in the bedroom with her tea when she went back. She slid beneath the quilt, smiling when he sat down beside her and handed her the cup. 'This is what I call room service.'

'So long as I'm the only one providing it, that's OK.' He kissed her quickly then nodded at the cup. 'Drink up before you spill it all over you.'

'Hmm, I'd need another shower then, wouldn't I?' she said, smiling smugly when she saw his eyes darken with passion.

'Yes, you would.' Another kiss before he reluctantly drew back. 'I've just seen Heather. She was down by the river when I went for a walk.'

'Is she all right?' Gemma asked, waiting for the pang of nerves that would surely hit her at mention of his ex-fiancée. It didn't happen and she smiled, delighted that she was as confident of his love as she'd thought she was. 'Come on, then, tell me what she said.'

'Apparently, she's met someone in London, a guy called Archie. From what I could gather she's mad about him but isn't sure how he feels about her.'

'Really? So what did you say to her?'

'That she should follow her heart and see where it leads her.' He laughed when she gasped. 'See, I'm giving out advice to the lovelorn now—how amazing is that?'

'Unbelievable,' she retorted, chuckling.

'Unbelievable?' His brows rose as he took the cup from her. 'Are you implying that I'm not in touch with my emotions?'

'Well, you do usually prefer a more reasoned approach,' she countered.

'I'm not sure how to take that,' he retorted, scooping her into his arms. 'I hope you're not implying that I'm a cold fish.'

'Not all of the time, no,' she began then laughed when he tickled her. 'Ross, no! Stop it, you pest!'

'Is that any way to speak to the man you love?' He tickled her again until she was squirming in his arms. Bending, he kissed her on the lips then drew back, one brow quirking. 'Still think I'm a pest?'

'No-o-o-o…you might just have redeemed yourself,' she whispered, looping her arms round his neck. There followed a very satisfactory interlude and Gemma sighed when he finally raised his head. 'I must call you names more often.'

'It's fun, isn't it?' He kissed her gently. 'Everything is fun when we do it together, Gemma. That's why I want to make sure that we never have to be apart. I know it may seem a bit soon to ask you this, but will you marry me? You don't have to give me your answer right away just as long as you'll think about it.'

'There's nothing to think about. Of course I'll marry you, Ross. Just try and stop me!'

He let out a whoop of joy as he pulled her to him and

kissed her. Gemma closed her eyes as the world started to spin. Round and round it went, and at the very heart of it was Ross and their love for one another. That was what would keep them together, always keep them feeling this way.

'I love you so much,' he whispered. 'I never dreamed that I could find someone as perfect as you to spend my life with.'

'Me too,' she whispered, feeling her heart swell with happiness. Ross had found his perfect wife at last, and it was her!

Celebrate 100 years of pure reading pleasure with Mills & Boon®

To mark our centenary, each month we're publishing a special 100th Birthday Edition. These celebratory editions are packed with extra features and include a FREE bonus story.

Plus, you have the chance to enter a fabulous monthly prize draw. See 100th Birthday Edition books for details.

Now that's worth celebrating!

September 2008

Crazy about her Spanish Boss by Rebecca Winters
Includes FREE bonus story
Rafael's Convenient Proposal

November 2008

**The Rancher's Christmas Baby
by Cathy Gillen Thacker**
Includes FREE bonus story *Baby's First Christmas*

December 2008

One Magical Christmas by Carol Marinelli
Includes FREE bonus story *Emergency at Bayside*

Look for Mills & Boon® 100th Birthday Editions at your favourite bookseller or visit
www.millsandboon.co.uk

FREE!

4 Books
and a surprise gift!

We would like to take this opportunity to thank you for reading this Mills & Boon® book by offering you the chance to take FOUR more specially selected titles from the Medical™ series absolutely FREE! We're also making this offer to introduce you to the benefits of the Mills & Boon® Book Club™—

- ★ **FREE home delivery**
- ★ **FREE gifts and competitions**
- ★ **FREE monthly Newsletter**
- ★ **Exclusive Mills & Boon Book Club offers**
- ★ **Books available before they're in the shops**

Accepting these FREE books and gift places you under no obligation to buy, you may cancel at any time, even after receiving your free shipment. Simply complete your details below and return the entire page to the address below. You don't even need a stamp!

YES! Please send me 4 free Medical books and a surprise gift. I understand that unless you hear from me, I will receive 6 superb new titles every month for just £2.99 each, postage and packing free. I am under no obligation to purchase any books and may cancel my subscription at any time. The free books and gift will be mine to keep in any case.

M8ZEF

Ms/Mrs/Miss/Mr .... Initials ....

Surname ....
BLOCK CAPITALS PLEASE

Address ....

....

.... Postcode ....

Send this whole page to:
UK: FREEPOST CN81, Croydon, CR9 3WZ